Sitting up, he got the rifle and held it out in front of him aiming it right toward her head. "Get up!" he ordered, hitting her leg with the barrel. She pushed herself across the floor to the corner where he was indicating, looking up into his dark eyes. With a terrible calm she knew she was about to die. All she had worked for to escape this man had been for nothing. How had her life come around full circle?

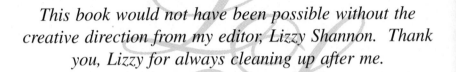

This book would not have been possible without the creative direction from my editor, Lizzy Shannon. Thank you, Lizzy for always cleaning up after me.

All charterers in this book have no existence outside the imagination of the author and have no relation whatsoever to anyone bearing the same name or names. They are not even distantly inspired by any individual known or unknown to the author, and all incidents are pure invention.

Lavender Skies

Alison White

PROLOGUE

The judge let the gavel fall on the large oak desk in front of him, calling the courtroom to order. Small whispers still permeated the air as he asked the presiding juror to stand.

Shea sat quietly in her seat, her knuckles white from gripping the arm of her chair too tightly. She was unable to silence the sobs that kept erupting from within her. Her father's fate now rested with the twelve people who sat in the jurors' box. His peers, but to her they were just strangers. Strangers who knew nothing about him, other than what they heard in the testimony, and the hideous accounts of the trial that were blasted all over the front pages of the paper. They knew nothing about her father's past but would now decide his future. Hell, they'd be deciding the whole family's future.

The judge tapped the desktop again to quiet the few whispers that still continued; then asked the defendant to stand. Shea watched her dad slowly rise from his seat, smoothing the suit that now hung loosely from his hollow frame. The stress from the past year had taken its toll on Jim Parks, a normally sturdy individual.

Nature had been good to him despite his five feet, eleven inch height. He'd been blessed with a muscular stature that seemed to survive the normal maladies of adulthood, but a form as strong as his, withered under the strains of coarse examination. His brawny physique stood a fraction of what it was. The sandy-blonde hair, which had always possessed a radiant luster, looked ragged and dull. His normal azure blue eyes palled, were now cast downward.

Shea thought about the stranger that had brought them to this point. The man they all thought they knew, an indisputable pillar of the community.

When Jim met Harvey Castleton it was an immediate attraction.

Harvey's dental practice in Albany thrived and he was looking for young blood. His clientele consisted of local political figures, the cream of the crop in every social circle. Jim jumped at the chance to join his team when Harvey offered him the deal of the century. He would work by commission until he could get enough collateral to buy into the partnership. Jim still owed thousands in student loans; this seemed like the perfect opportunity to pay them off while at the same time building his practice.

Soon after Jim started, another partner was added. Mark Lee, like Jim, was fresh out of school. The three hit it off wonderfully. The appointment books continued to grow, and soon Jim was making a comfortable living.

Who could ever have known what was going on behind the closed doors of their partner's office? It was the scandal that rocked their little community, setting many of the townsfolk tongues a-wagging with speculation. Everyone had an opinion on the subject that caused a media frenzy in their sleepy little neighborhood. An informant had tipped the police off to illegal drug transactions taking place at Castleton, Lee and Parks on Delaware Avenue. After obtaining the proper warrants, the police raided the offices, sending patients scurrying out to the street. All three men were arrested, now they waited for the verdict.

Two days ago, Mark Lee was found not guilty on all charges. Although Harvey admitted to working solely by himself in the conspiracy, mysterious papers showed up in both Jim Parks' and Mark Lee's personal files. The trials were established to fully clear their names from any wrong doing.

Worse than the trial was the relentless scrutiny of the media. Journalists had camped outside their door, waiting, for the slightest juicy piece of dirt to report on. The writers had worked their ruthless, black magic so well, the publicity took its toll on the practice's clientele. Business dwindled to a scant existence. People just didn't want to be associated with a place accused of such atrocities. Even some of Jim's closest friends faded into nonexistence.

With no money coming in and mounting lawyer's bills, Jim was forced to sell their house. They sold off most of their assets to support them during the rough time.

In the courtroom, Shea turned to look at Billy. He had been watching her and winked when she saw him. She smiled slightly, returning her attention to the jury. Billy, her one true love, her pillar of strength. He was the one who stuck by her during the entire agonizing ordeal. She was comforted by his presence. Today more than ever his steadfast devotion radiated as he sat there, his confident air shining from him in a warm glow of light. Shea took solace in his adoration, for she knew Billy loved her. It was the only thing she was sure of anymore.

Shea's mom placed her hand over hers. Shea clasped it tightly, holding it close to her heart. She looked at her mom's tear-stained face. Only a trace of her alluring beauty had been untouched by the devastation of the past months.

A gruff voice demanded from the podium, "Has the jury made a decision?"

"We have." The older gentleman who answered swayed on his fragile frame, holding onto the ledge of the jurors' box for support. His tall, lanky form was bent over, displaying his obvious old age. His hands trembled as he tilted his glasses up to read through the bifocals, holding the piece of paper out in front of him.

Shea leaned forward to squelch the knot in her stomach. She gripped a tissue firmly in her fist.

The elderly man cleared his throat before reading the verdict. "We, the jury, find James S. Parks not guilty on all charges."

Shea was holding so tight she almost didn't hear the words. When they finally sank in, she bolted from her chair, throwing her arms around her mother. Jim jumped up and hugged his attorney as the courtroom burst into applause. Billy came over. Grabbing Shea, he pulled her close, kissing her over and over. She cried uncontrollably against his chest as relief rushed over her.

Jim turned to his family. "I could never have gotten through this with out the two of you." Tears formed in his eyes.

People approached from all sides to hug and clap Jim on the back. The jury came up one by one to congratulate them, the presiding juror taking Jim's hand and pressing it into his. "None of us ever thought you had anything to do with this. We just want you to know how happy we are that this messy ordeal is over. Now that they know the truth maybe the newspaper will write a decent story about you. Oh, and can I get some dental work done?" he added with a smile.

Jim pulled the man by his hand and hugged him close. Tears of jubilation ran freely down his face. Dozens of reporters waited outside the courthouse for them. Jim was tight-lipped, as he pushed his family through the clamoring crowds to the car that had been waiting for them. They drove off with a host of reporters on their trail. But Jim refused to speak to them; they had done the most damage and they didn't deserve to get the victory story.

◆　　　◆　　　◆

Shea sat quietly listening to the slow beeping of the heart monitor. She watched the green line moving up and down in rhythm to her mother's breathing. A machine kept her mother alive now, tubes coming out of every inch of her body.

Shea pressed her mother's hand closely to her lips, choking back the sobs begging to get out. Her eyes were dry, there were no more tears. The exhaustion was taking hold and there was little energy left for emotions. How could this all be happening? she wondered. Just four short months ago her family was celebrating her father's triumphant acquittal. Things were finally starting to turn around for them. Her dad's business had picked up and there was extra money again.

Shea and her mom had gone shopping for new clothes, like they had done in the old days. When they got home, the house was oddly quiet. Going to her room while her mother looked for her husband, Shea had just started to change when she heard her mom scream. She ran to see what was wrong and found her dad spread out on the bedroom floor. Calling the paramedics, she started CPR but it was too late. Jim Parks lay dead of a massive heart attack: the final outcome from all the stress that had been built up over the year.

Her mother, Abbey, was devastated. She tried to be strong for Shea, but she never got over the death of her one and only true love.

When they found a lump at the base of Abbey's neck, her doctor sent her straight to the hospital. A biopsy confirmed the grim truth and they operated immediately. Abbey tried to handle the chemotherapy as best she could, but she was still weak from the despair of her husband's death. The doctors had high hopes, but Abbey had lost her will to live. No doctor could ever diagnose what Shea already knew. Her mom lay dying of a broken heart.

Shea moved her lips next to her mothers ear. "It's okay, mom," she whispered softly, "I know you love daddy too much to ever leave him. I love you mom, I know you love me too. I understand and will always love you. Go to him... tell him I love him."

She kissed her mom's forehead. "Good-bye, mom. You don't have to suffer anymore." Shea put her mom's hand back down on the bed and went to the door. She turned and blew a kiss to her mom before she left the room. Shea walked to the lounge where Billy and Aunt Victoria waited. Vicki was Abbey's older sister and Shea's favorite aunt. She'd come up as soon as Abbey was diagnosed and had stayed to help out. Shea gave her aunt a disheartened nod and Vicki hurried off down the hall. Shea slumped into the couch next to Billy, who took her in his arms and held her close. He could feel her soft sobs against his neck. So much had happened to her in the past few months and Billy felt helpless to stop her pain. All he could do now was hold her and let her cry.

When Vicki appeared a few minutes later, Shea knew her mother was gone. Abbey was at peace, she thought. Although she would miss her mom terribly, Shea knew she was with her beloved. Vicki joined them on the couch and Shea put her arms around her. Shea adored her Aunt Vicki, and she'd been there through all the tough times. Together they cried.

"She's at peace now," Shea finally whispered.

"Yes, she's finally gone to see her true love."

Shea looked at her in surprise. Her aunt knew the truth about her mother's demise.

CHAPTER ONE

My Dearest Shea,

Where has the time gone? Seems like just yesterday we were fighting over toys in the back yard. Now here we are, closing the chapter on one life and opening a new one.

Whatever we do we'll do it together. I know you need to get your degree: I support you one hundred percent. I will miss you dearly while you're gone, but I will call and write every day.

Our best days are ahead of us. Together we will conquer new worlds and build vast empires. The world is ours to have. Together we will have everything.

People said it would never last... even now they have their doubts. No one will ever know because only we understand the depth of our love. When you get home we will continue our journey.

Remember Shea, I love you for eternity, beyond eternity and past the heavens. You are my life forever.

Love Always, Billy

Shea closed her yearbook and placed it on the vanity. Running her fingers over the insignia on the cover, she remembered what they'd been through. It was hard to believe it was all over. Just two weeks ago her life was a flurry of finals and graduation preparations. And now, a new beginning.

Shea pulled her massive abundance of platinum curls into a pony tail holder, letting them fall loosely over one shoulder. In the mirror she searched her tepid eyes and sighed, their brilliant sea green color diminished from long hours of studying. However, her skin had acquired an opulent golden hue from the long hours she'd spent in the sun. When most others worried about the harsh effects of the early summer sun, Shea seemed immune to those first summer burns. It had been her friends' idea to ease the drudgery of studying. They would meet in small groups, equipped with not

1

much more than a two piece swimsuit and suntan oil, and spend the afternoons quizzing each other. However, most of these assemblages turned into gossip sessions about their peers or a teacher they all thought was deserving of a merciless bashing. They never got much accomplished, and Shea often found herself calling Billy in a desperate plea to help her catch up.

Billy had always been her knight in shining armor. For as long as she could remember he had been coming to her rescue. They had grown up living next door to each other. Although they fought bitterly most of the time, if any of the other neighborhood boys pulled such pranks, they'd often find themselves subject to a thrashing at the hands of Billy, for only he was allowed such liberties. That was the way it was. The neighborhood bullies knew it and never questioned it.

Things remained that way until the summer before middle school. Shea had gone to Florida with her parents to visit her aunt and uncle, who were both doctors. Shea loved her Aunt Vicki. She was an eccentric with strange ideas about most everything, but Shea thought she was cool as she promised to take her to Disney World, and a bunch of other places.

Billy accepted this separation with reluctance, but they both promised to write everyday and Shea sent him a postcard from every new place she visited.

When their car finally rode past Billy's house a few days before school started, he ran across the field to greet her, excited to show her the scrap book he had put together from all their correspondence. He ran up to the car, stopping dead in front of her. She had changed! He stared in confusion. What had happened to the Shea who left him standing in that exact spot only two months before? Her figure had taken on a new shape... had her aunt or uncle performed some sort of operation on her?

There were slight swells where there had never been anything before and her cardboard features had softened to tender curves. This new Shea left Billy perplexed as well as giving him a funny feeling inside he couldn't make head nor tail of. Even though Shea sounded and acted the same toward him he knew things were

2

somehow different. She now commanded a different type of attention. No longer did he feel the urge to push her down in the mud just to see her cry, for the new Shea needed more delicate treatment. Even though she didn't act any different, somehow he understood that never again would he torment her in the customary manner he was used to, and it terrified him.

It was obvious to Billy when school started again that he wasn't the only one to notice the transformation. He wasn't comfortable with the reaction this brought out in him and he liked it even less coming from his friends. He also despaired that he had to run to Shea's rescue more and more, costing him countless friendships.

There were a lot more boys in their new school than there were in the neighborhood and he didn't command the same kind of respect he'd grown used to as the turf leader. There were new rules, which Billy was not in control of. It scared him that Shea who had always been what he considered his possession was now fair game.

Yes, this new Shea was definitely more complicated. His feelings about her didn't help matters any, for no matter how he looked at it he couldn't hate her. Their friendship began to change in ways he couldn't comprehend.

Shea showed no interest in the many suitors that camped out by her locker. The reaction of the other boys scared her so much she found herself clinging to Billy more. Shea thought of her metamorphosis as a curse and wished she could just be left alone. Except for Billy that is. More and more she found herself on his doorstep with her hair all curly, even wearing makeup when she could sneak it past her mom.

Naomi would answer the door with a smile at Shea's innocence. "Billy's up in his room," she would announce and Shea would be off up the stairs in a flash.

Most of their afternoons were spent in Billy's room listening to music. Billy would show her his latest model, Shea pretending she was interested just to keep his attention.

Neither parents paid much attention to the growing passion that was going on with Billy and Shea. The two became inseparable. It

3

didn't stop other boys from asking Shea out, although they all knew what her answer would be. They tried anyway, but Shea was definitely not available and she made it very clear. Billy himself had caught a few eyes, besides being the son of one of the wealthiest families in the area he had grown into a very handsome young man. He rapidly sprouted to almost six feet tall. His wavy brown hair and natural tan set his robin's egg blue eyes off to perfection. But Billy had eyes for only one person.

The relationship eventually sparked some concern with the families. Soon the Kendall's and the Parks were meeting to figure out a way to get Billy and Shea to see other people. They didn't feel it was healthy for the two to be so concerned with each other. Shea's mom encouraged her to go out with the myriad of boys that called their house, even going as far as to invite a couple for dinner, but Shea skipped out, (with Billy of course,) leaving her parents sitting at the dinner table awkwardly trying to explain Shea's absence.

This was not to be outdone by Billy's parents, who set Billy up on a date with Sarah, Shea's own cousin! When it was time to meet Sarah, Jake went upstairs to get his son. When Billy didn't answer the knock, Jake opened the door to find the curtain blowing in the wind. Billy had sneaked out to climb down the porch column.

Sarah was left standing in the hall, her hair done up in a twist and wearing a wool skirt and boots. "Oh, those two are hopeless," she sputtered, storming out of the house.

Jake and Naomi realized Sarah was right. They were only hurting their children with their actions and decided to leave fate alone. They figured nature would take its course. Besides it could be worse. Jake and Naomi adored Shea and Abbey, and Jim treated Billy like he was their own. They knew they should be thankful. Billy and Shea never got into trouble and they were both on the honor roll at school.

Abbey did sit Shea down and talk to her. Shea assured her mother she and Billy weren't having sex, and if they decided to she would tell her mom so she could go on the pill. The two also

4

promised their parents they would go to college and not rush into marriage right after high school. With their parents' minds set at ease, Billy and Shea went about their lives together and most everyone left them alone.

There was still the crowd of suitors that flocked to Shea's locker every day, and the occasional girl who focused on the Kendall money, but everyone knew they were an item.

Shea must have been deep in thought because she didn't hear the bedroom door open behind her.

"Shea!" The voice came so sharply it made the hairs raise on the back of her neck.

"Oh, Auntie Caroline," Shea spun round on the seat. "You frightened me."

Caroline made her way across the room to the window and pulled the curtains back, closing the window so hard it made Shea jump. It was then she saw the huge, black clouds gathering in the distance. Her aunt made her way past the bed to close the other window. She stood looking down into the huge back yard where Sarah's graduation party was in full swing. There were yellow and white tents set up all over; hopefully they would suffice the crowds when the rain finally hit.

Shea suppressed a smile. She knew her aunt was cringing at the thought of all those bawdy teenagers taking over the house. Caroline had always been such a snob, this house her pride and joy. She only allowed the finest of everything to be displayed and never tired of boring her guests with her endless boasting. Her life was a frenzy of never-ending shopping sprees. Shea almost burst out laughing with the thought of it. All those drunk, rowdy teens rambling through her house. After all, it doesn't take a genius to know that intoxicated youths and Waterford crystal don't mix.

"What are you doing up here all alone?" Caroline finally asked, letting the curtain fall back into place.

Shea nervously dug at her nails. She always hated these confrontations with her aunt. Besides she didn't want to tell her the truth, that she'd become bored with Sarah's snooty friends bragging about the new cars mommy and daddy were going to buy them for graduation.

5

"I needed to freshen up," she replied casually, studying the torn skin at the base of her fingernail. She could hear her aunt's indignant sigh of disgust. Caroline always had a way of diminishing any normal thoughts and feelings to nothing but an enormous over-reaction to an exaggerated imagination.

"You've been up here for over an hour," insisted Caroline, winding the gold Rolex on her wrist.

Shea squirmed, crossing her arms in front of her. "I've been up here that long?" She gave a silly grin, not thoroughly convinced it was a full hour. But it didn't matter, it was long enough for her aunt to come looking and that's what bothered her most. She silently kicked herself for not having the sense to leave the house altogether. Now she had to stay and endure Aunt Caroline's end-less barrage of questions and snide comments about the fact Shea had practically abandoned the party.

Aunt Caroline had an uncanny knack for talking down to people. Even those she felt herself equal to, which weren't many. She would berate and criticize until her target wanted to scream with frustration. She especially used this technique when she wanted to get her own way. Shea's Uncle John was a saint in most peoples' eyes. To their mystification, he had learned to put up with Caroline's temper tantrums ages ago. Caroline could harp forever about what was wrong with this, or how that should have been fixed a certain way. People usually gave in to her demands just to shut her up.

"I guess I must have gotten lost in thought." Shea's words tumbled out before she could catch them.

Caroline sniffed and walked over to the mirror to comb her hair, tousled by the gusts of wind that were bringing the storm. Shea felt a twinge as she watched. From the back Caroline looked so much like her mother. Both sisters were tall and slender. Shea wished she could have been built more like them, but she took after her Aunt Vicki. Although she loved Vicki, she didn't relish the attributes passed on to her from that side of the family. Even here cousin, Sarah was tall and slender. Shea looked down at her own short, buxom figure heaving under the pressure of her over-developed breasts.

6

Caroline removed the barrettes she was arranging in her hair and turned to face Shea. "Oh, honestly. I swear, Shea. Is thinking all you Parks' do?"

Her voice slapped Shea with its intensity. She shook her head and let her curls fall restlessly in place.

"I worry about you. You ought to be careful," continued Caroline with halfhearted conviction. "You know that's what...."

"What?" Shea stopped her mid sentence. "What were you going to say, Aunt Caroline?" She swung around the side of the bed and grabbed the post. "That's how my father died? That's what you were going to say, wasn't it?" Shea swallowed the tears that were trying to get out.

"Well, we all know it's the truth," Caroline spewed, so matter of fact.

As if that's what everyone actually believed had happened. Shea knew better.

"If he had joined your uncle's dental practice...." Caroline shook her head in disgust. "He always had to try and prove something." She turned back toward the mirror. Shea could tell she was crying.

Shea knew the story well. Her father and Uncle John were roommates in college, and became very close friends. They talked about starting their own practice when they graduated. That was before they met the girls. Caroline had been seeing Jim, who insisted on finding a girl for John so they could double-date. Caroline begged her sister to help out and very reluctantly Abbey agreed. When Jim and Abbey met face to face in the restaurant that night, they knew it was love. Jim called Abbey shortly after, but Abbey refused to go out with him because he was dating her sister. She knew they weren't getting along, but it was the principle of the matter. Jim broke up with Caroline and soon he and Abbey were an item. Caroline was outraged at first, but soon forgave her sister. She had to admit the four of them did have some great times together. When John called and asked her out she couldn't refuse, suggesting they all go out together. The four of them were a team again.

7

They had a double-wedding, and set up house next door to each other. Even Shea and Sarah were born only a few weeks apart. Things went well, and when the guys graduated from college, they both went to work for other people. They still discussed opening a practice together, although increasingly Jim didn't think it was a good idea to set up a business with a family member. He still had no idea where he would get that kind of money. John's dad had already offered to set him up, but Jim's parents were not wealthy by any means.

He decided to join an already thriving practice in Albany. The deal was perfect. He would work there for five years with money taken out of his check each week to put toward his partnership. After five years, he would become a full-fledged partner. Jim got along well with both of the partners and it was great finally getting a real paycheck. They had a large clientele that continued to grow.

When Jim announced his intention to join Harvey's practice at a family dinner, he received stunned looks from everyone, but no one was more shocked than John. The families remained relatively friendly. But after the bomb was dropped, John and Caroline displayed a coolness toward Jim and Abbey that was apparent at all the get-togethers. Jim knew they felt betrayed, but he had to do what he felt was best for his family.

Shea and Sarah got along with cool regard for each other, too. They never actually disliked each other, but they didn't have much in common. Sarah went to private school and did all the things most rich kids did. Sarah wasn't a normal child, according to the opinion of the neighborhood kids. When she was five her mom carted her off to private school. Every morning while all the children waited for the bus, Caroline would drive by with Sarah sitting like a princess beside her. There were a lot of similarities between Sarah and her mother, although Sarah would staunchly deny it. Shea never really had much to talk about with Sarah, so they both joined their own crowd of peers, remaining friendly on a superficial level.

Shea glared at her aunt through the tears that finally escaped. "My father was a good man. I don't have to stand here and listen to this." She turned and grabbed her purse from the vanity.

Caroline laughed out loud. "He was mixed up with criminals, for God's sake!"

Shea spun around so fast, her purse flew out almost hitting her aunt. Secretly she wished it had. "He had nothing to do with that and you know it! He wasn't even aware it was happening." Shea's voice was icy. She stared her aunt down, waiting for the next attack.

"Oh, please. Everyone in town knew what was happening," spat Caroline sarcastically.

Shea fumed silently. If she hadn't been sure before, she was certain now, she hated this woman. Hated her with all her heart and soul. How could Aunt Caroline talk to her like this knowing how hard her father's death had been on her? And how could that woman even think her dad would knowingly get involved with a drug pusher, and knowingly put his family through that mess? Her dad had suffered hard through the whole ordeal. Slowly his patients dropped away, then the investigators, hoards of them searching every square inch of his office, digging through his files like he was a criminal himself. His and the family's privacy was invaded mercilessly. Then came the questions and the trial. Her dad began to look pale. He endured hours of interrogations. As the trial continued, he was badgered and forced to testify. When the stress became too much the doctor put him on valium. How could Caroline think anyone would ever want to put themselves through such torture?

Following the trial things settled down after about a year. Jim and Mark had to work hard to rebuild the business. Through it all where had Aunt Caroline been? It didn't take Shea long to find out who'd been spreading those horrific rumors about her dad. When he first joined Harvey's practice, the scorn was obvious. Uncle John had tried to patch things up many times, but Caroline would always step in, preventing it before he was able to. Even after her father's death it was Aunt Vicki who came to New York to comfort Abbey, not Caroline.

Shea had been so strong for her mom that it wasn't until the day of the funeral that she really allowed herself to let go. When she finally did, it was Billy again who took care of her. He rocked her gently, softly caressing her hair. She collapsed on his bed as the violent shudders overtook her. Billy had lain down next to her, holding on as tight as he could. They clung to each other until Shea had cried herself to sleep.

When Shea looked up, she saw her aunt's shoulders shaking, racked with sobs. "You know Shea, you weren't the only one who lost someone in the deal," Caroline blurted out before the sobs took control again. "I lost my sister. My dear, sweet wonderful sister." Her words were barely audible. She turned, resting her hands on the dresser. "I tried to warn your mom about your dad. Oh, how I tried, but she wouldn't listen." Her voice was almost a whisper. "And because of him she's...."

"No!" Shea backed away from her aunt. "You're wrong, Aunt Caroline." Her voice cracked. "How can you say such a thing? He loved mom. You're crazy!" She grabbed her yearbook from the vanity and ran from the room. Flying down the marble stairs, she ran straight to her car, not bothering to close the front door or say good-bye to her cousin.

Revving the engine, Shea peeled out of the driveway. She tore along the cornfields, thinking about what her aunt had said. When she found a clearing she pulled the car over and wept bitterly. She wished it was Aunt Victoria that lived here.

When Vicki had come to stay with Shea after her mom's death, despite the circumstances, Vicki made it easier for Shea. She talked with her about Billy and relationships. She stayed on until all the matters were taken care of and Shea had gone back to school. Vicki let her borrow clothes and jewelry. When it was finally time for her to go, Shea was devastated. She would miss her aunt terribly, but she wanted to stay in school where she was. The inevitable choice to become Shea's guardian was Aunt Caroline, since Shea's dad had no family in the area. Caroline lived outside the school district, the line running between the two houses. Shea went to court to get permission to stay with her friend Lee Ann. There was plenty of room and it would be best for Shea to graduate with her own class. The court granted her permission but stated that Aunt Caroline would remain her legal guardian.

Shea dried her eyes with the T-shirt Billy had left in her front seat. She headed over to the nursery where he worked. His parents owned it. Jake was getting on in years and hadn't been well at all; after Billy graduated he put him to work learning all aspects of the business so he could take over. This put Billy's plans for college off for a while, but it was okay with him. He would be gaining valuable experience and he decided he could get his degree at a later date.

Billy had been working long hours and Shea knew she'd find him there. She swung her car into a parking space near the front entrance and hopped out. The clouds were almost overhead, looking like they might burst any minute.

When she entered, Billy was busy stacking bags of fertilizer. She stormed through the warehouse, ignoring a hello that Billy's younger brother Michael yelled out as she passed. Michael still had a year left in school, and would have the luxury of going off to college, as it was Billy's responsibility to run the shop.

Spotting Shea, Billy crossed the warehouse to meet her. He gave her a peck on the cheek and looked longingly at her. He could see the tear stains around her eyes. "Your aunt called," he said, leading her to the office.

She finally noticed Michael and turned with a slight wave before disappearing into the office. Billy laid the gloves he wore on a stack of seed that was sitting just inside the office door. When they got inside he shut them in. Shea propped herself up on the big oak desk and leaned against the wall, looking down at the well she had dug out of her cuticle earlier. "What did dear Auntie Caroline want?" she asked sullenly. Shea could feel the rage from the afternoon tryst building up in her again.

"She was worried about you."

"*Caroline?*"

"That must have been a humdinger of a fight you two had. She sounded like she was crying." Billy got up to fix some coffee. He could tell she was still bothered by the incident. Giving her the cup, he lifted her head to him. "Care to talk about it?"

11

"There's nothing to talk about. Aunt Caroline was being her normal, selfish inconsiderate self."

"Your aunt is a bit of a...." " He stopped, searching for the right word.

"A bitch," finished Shea. "She's nothing but a bitch and everyone knows it. Now, we've got more important things to talk about. Are we still going camping this weekend?"

Billy was surprised by the sudden change of conversation. He sat down in the chair in front of her. "Hmm, nice view," he grinned, staring at the spot between her legs.

Shea swiftly sat up, crossing her legs. She put down the empty coffee cup. "How about Lake George? I want to go someplace different. Don't you, Billy?" She gave him a cheery smile.

Billy sat back in the chair, still perplexed about her sudden change. "Lake George is fine with me," he answered carefully, scrutinizing her tone.

"Get serious, Billy! You've got to have an opinion."

"I told you Lake George is fine with me."

"Well, now I know you're lying, you little scamp. You've always said it was too crowded. If you're not going to make a decision I guess I'll have to. Let's see." She stared into space as if the answer was printed on the wall.

Billy watched her, his hands crossed with his chin resting on them.

"There's Sacandaga. And..." Her head dropped as she choked, "She implied my dad killed my mom."

Billy surged from his seat to hold her. The tears came out in a steady flow and Shea covered her face with her hands. "I was wondering when you were going to get to this," he said, soothing her.

"I hate her, Billy. I swear, I hate her."

He rubbed her hair. "Shea, you can't take what your aunt said as the truth. She has always been a little strange. Look, even my parents say that." He handed her a tissue and she dried her eyes. Taking another one he held it to her nose. "Blow!" he commanded teasingly.

Suddenly Shea fell back on the desk in a fit of laughter. "Know what's scary?" she gulped, "Sarah's just like her."

They both burst out laughing. Billy slid up on the desk to lie beside Shea. When she turned on her side Billy brushed up against her.

"Billy?" Shea was taken aback. "Is this the way you console someone?" she whispered, "or are you taking advantage of a grieving woman?" She suddenly got a funny feeling inside and sat up with a jolt. She knew what it was because she had been feeling it more and more when she was with Billy. She fought it each time, wondering if she'd be strong enough the next. Leaning back against the wall, she let her legs drape over Billy's. He took her hand and pressed it against the bulge in his jeans.

Pulling her hand away with a jerk, she snapped, "I thought we said we were going to wait until I was out of college?"

"We don't have to do anything," he replied softly. "I just need you to know how badly I want you."

She looked away from him.

"Shea." He sat up, swinging his legs down over the side of the desk and hopped off. "Are you okay?"

"Yeah." She didn't look at him.

"What's wrong?"

"I've been thinking about it myself," she stammered. After a pause, she looked at him. "Billy, I don't want to wait anymore."

He didn't hide his surprise. "Seriously?"

She nodded. "I don't want to go off to college without taking a part of you with me. I love you Billy, and I'm ready now. I want to seal our love for one another. This weekend."

Billy stared. "What about getting pregnant, and the marriage thing and all that?"

"We'll use protection. Billy, I'm not going to be less in love with you just because we're not married!"

Billy often thought it was fortunate she was going away to college, because more and more those urges gnawed at him. He found it hard to restrain himself when he was with her.

Reaching for her, he gripped Shea's head, crushing her lips beneath his. She kissed him back with a passionate fury. Both longed for the weekend when they would finally seal their love.

CHAPTER TWO

Kevin strode out of the airport and looked around him. Not much had changed, he thought to himself. But that didn't surprise him. He squinted into the hazy sky, then searched through the pockets of his jean-jacket for his sunglasses. Walking to the edge of the sidewalk, he looked up and down for the bus that would take him to the rental car agency. Storm clouds accumulated not far off. Kevin hoped the shuttle arrived before the rain hit. He could feel the soft, brown waves of his hair start to wrinkle under the intense humidity. Wiping beads of sweat from his forehead, he opened the paper he had been holding under his arm. He scanned the headlines again. They still made him as angry as when he read them the first time.

He took one last drag off the cigarette that hung from his lips, then flicked it to the ground. The smoke billowed out in one long, steady stream, carried away by the balmy breeze. He diverted his attention back to the article and read it again. '*Jake Kendall Retires, Leaves Business to Eldest Son.*' The words stung bitterly. Kevin crumpled the paper in a fury, stuffing it into the garbage can. He paced feverishly up and down the walkway until anger overwhelmed him. Kicking the cement garbage can with a frenzied pounding, he cursed at the pain that jolted through his foot and up his leg.

He couldn't believe his dad would do this to him. It was obvious which son he considered his eldest, but he still couldn't believe his dad would so blatantly betray him. It was beyond him how his dad could pretend he didn't exist, but Kevin would make sure his dad would never forget him again. He hadn't known his dad went down to the paper the following day to correct the mistake. Neither did Kevin see the retraction, for he left for the airport as soon as he'd read the story.

He'd ordered a subscription to the hometown paper when he was in prison. It helped him keep tabs on his family's business. The town was small and the Kendalls were one of the more prominent families in the area. And Kevin was a member of that prominent family whether his father wanted to acknowledge him or not. Kevin was only glad he had seen the article; it gave him enough time to get back into town to claim what was rightfully his. It was more his than his half-brothers. After all, his mom and dad started the business together. It was a product of both of their hard work.

Sprinkles of rain started falling and the sky turned a dark gray. Looking at his watch, Kevin swore again. He gazed out over the parking lot in vain for the shuttle. The rain started to come down harder, so he walked back under the eves of the building to wait.

When the shuttle finally pulled up in front of the airport, Kevin ran through the downpour and climbed in. As the van took him to the local rental car agency, he leaned back against the window, settling the anger still brewing inside him. He pondered about the past few years when he thought he and his dad were finally making amends. Kevin had been thrown in jail this last time, about ten years ago. When it had first happened, his dad would barely talk to him. He'd helped his son out of so many scrapes before, but even he couldn't help him out of the last escapade. Kevin had been busted for armed robbery.

His problems had started before he was out of high school. He barely made graduation and even when he did, the army was waiting for him when he got out. It was the height of the Vietnam War and Kevin received his draft notice. As hard as it was for his father to let him go. Jake knew the discipline would be good for him. Still suffering from the loss of his wife, Jake was in no condition to take care of a hard-to-handle youth. He still had his daughter Brenda to think about, and frankly, Jake hated exposing her to the sordid shenanigans Kevin seemed to be involved with all the time. It was a never-ending battle between father and son. Still, Jake loved Kevin dearly and sent him a letter the same day he left for boot camp.

The army didn't change a thing. When Kevin got back home,

his troubles escalated. Jake tried his best, even seeking the help of the best psychologists in the area to talk with Kevin. His wife's death had been hard on both the kids, but Kevin seemed to take it the hardest.

Kevin and Brenda had a near-perfect childhood. Their mother never had to work, so she spent all her time doting on the two children. Brenda, being as independent as she was didn't need much tending to, but Kevin ate up his mom's attention. He never had to try very hard, for his mom was always willing to cater to his every whim. All in all he had a happy childhood. Pretty idealistic by any kid's standards.

He was eleven when it happened. It was late one snowy night. His mom took classes at a college in town; she was on her way home when a truck driver spun out of control and hit her. It happened fast, both drivers were killed instantly. Kevin's perfect little world came crashing down on top of him. The person he loved so dearly, the one who adored him was gone. He was shattered. How could God be so cruel as to take away the only person who understood Kevin's needs? No one else could ever replace what he'd lost out on that dark, icy highway.

Life had always been so easy, now Kevin didn't know how to cope. His grades plummeted and he lost his enthusiasm for school. Little by little he stopped attending. When Jake caught wind of it, he ordered his son back to school and personally drove him every day to be sure he got there. He tried to be understanding of his son, often setting up chat sessions, so Kevin could discuss his feelings.

With no other way out, Kevin started causing trouble to get himself expelled. He didn't want to go to school, he hated it. This went on through the next six years. Jake was at his wits end, not knowing what else to do. He found it somewhat of a relief to have his son going off to the army.

The headlines in the paper only heightened what Kevin had felt for a long time. His dad wished he wasn't around, or worse, he preferred not to recognize him as his own. Whatever the answer, Kevin felt he had as much right to the family business as the other

17

children. He was the first son, his father could not deny that. No, his father *would* not deny him that. Of this Kevin was certain.

On one of his trips home, during leave, Kevin heard his dad was remarrying. He fumed when he learned the news but couldn't believe what he was told next. The man who cared so much about public appearance that he shipped his son off to the army to save himself from the embarrassment was marrying a woman half his age. Kevin's friends kidded him about it, which infuriated him even more. He wouldn't know how young she was until he actually met her. She was very beautiful, only two years older than Kevin himself.

Kevin never really got over his mother's death. This new woman only posed more problems. Again he felt betrayed by his dad. Even though it had been over eight years, Kevin could not accept his father's devotion to another woman. He went out of his way to let his father know he disapproved.

At the car rental lot, the agent handed Kevin the keys. "Here you are, Mr. Kendall. Your car is around the side of the building, the gold Pontiac." He made a circular motion with his finger to signal the way. Kevin nodded, following the directions.

Making his way out of the parking lot, he headed to the corner store. He bought a newspaper and quickly drove to a motel. When he settled in, he searched through the paper for a used car. He didn't want to waste his money on rentals and he was planning on being in town for a while anyway.

CHAPTER THREE

Shea bolted awake and looked at the clock. It was five thirty. Not quite dark yet although the rain clouds made it appear darker than it should be. A shrill ringing told her what had woken her. She ran to the phone, tripping over a shoe in the process.

"Hello!" Her voice came breathlessly as she pressed the receiver to her ear.

"Get me outa here!" A distressed voice came from the other end.

"Who is this?" Shea asked, concerned.

"It's Sylvie, silly."

Shea relaxed when she heard her laugh. "Sylvie, where are you?"

"I'm at home. You've got to get me out of here, before I go crazy."

"When did you get home?" Shea settled back on the bed, smiling. Sylvie went to boarding school in Connecticut, but they kept in touch throughout the year. Shea wrote about Billy and she, Sylvie telling her about the boys who lived in the dorms across the campus from her. Some of them 'tall, rugged and gorgeous,' others 'short, stocky and cute.' But all of them rich, rich, rich.

"I got in this afternoon, Shea. My mom invited the whole family over. Good God, they're driving me crazy."

"That bad, huh?"

"Ah! They're asking me all these questions like where are you going to college, are you dating anyone? Blah, blah, blah," she chimed mockingly.

Shea laughed hysterically. "At least you don't have to listen to, when are you and Billy going to come to your senses and see other people."

"You're still going with him?"

19

"See what I mean?" snorted Shea.

"Sorry, I promise I won't say that anymore." Sylvie sounded repentant. "Anyway, I called to see if you were busy tonight. Want to go to the Ice House?"

Shea thought for a moment. "Gosh, Sylvie, I haven't been to any of those places in so long. Does anybody still go there?"

The Ice ouse was a pizza and pool hall. A lot of the local teens hung out there. It was usually a good place to start an evening, see who was out, form small groups and go dancing in Albany.

"I called a couple of other people who said they'd meet us there. I just don't want to drive there alone, Shea."

"Okay, I'll go. Billy's been working so much, all he does is go home and fall asleep, anyway."

"He's at his dad's shop?"

"Yes, Jake hasn't been well. Billy's taking over the business."

"Girl, you are going to be one rich lady if you ever marry that guy."

"Of course I'm going to marry him, but I want to go to college first. Do you always have to think of things in monetary terms?"

"Oh, please Shea, spare me. You mean to tell me you don't think of the kind of house you'll be living in, or that you can buy any car your little heart desires?"

"Sylvie, those things are all nice, but I'm marrying Billy because I love him." She thought about those words, meaning them from the bottom of her heart. He was her everything.

"Oh, I know you two are hopeless. So I'll pick you up at seven, be waiting."

Shea hung up the phone and flipped on the radio. Singing along to Pat Benatar, she rummaged through the closet for something to wear. She settled on a white Indian gauze skirt with a matching blouse. Putting her white boots up next to the outfit, she headed for the shower.

She was just putting the finishing touches on her makeup when the phone rang again. Billy always called her when he was closing up. Shea looked at the clock, it was five after seven. Sylvie was late, of course, but it would give her time to talk to Billy before she went out. Answering the phone, she put on an alluring voice. "Jasmine's sex hot line."

"You really shouldn't do that, Shea." Billy sounded irritated.

"What if it wasn't me?"

"Billy, I know it's you, you always call me the same time every night."

"Sounds like that bothers you," he sniped.

"Of course not, don't be silly. What's gotten into you?"

"I don't know, Shea. It seems like we don't spend much time together anymore."

"Billy, you're working all the time. Is that my fault?"

"So you're saying it's mine? This is our future, Shea."

"Billy, I can't believe after our conversation this afternoon you can actually think anything is wrong."

"Well, I know you love me and all. I just wonder if you're getting bored with the relationship."

"Don't be ridiculous. No, I don't like that you work so much, but I also know you have to."

"You coming over tonight?" he asked hopefully.

"I can't. I'm going out with Sylvie, but I'll call you tomorrow and we can talk more about this."

From the window she saw Sylvie tear up the driveway, leaving a cloud of dust rising in the floodlight. She pounded on the horn impatiently.

"Look I gotta run, Billy. I'll talk to you in the morning."

"Do you love me?" he asked hesitantly.

"Of course I do. Now let me go. Sylvie's blowing the horn. She'll bother the neighbors if I don't stop her. I promise I'll call you in the morning." Shea hung up the phone, quickly grabbed her purse and rushed out the door.

Sylvie popped her head out the window. "Like my new wheels?" she asked, running her hands over the gold Mercedes.

"This is yours?" Shea asked, astonished.

"Well, actually it's my dad's, but it'll be mine until I leave for college."

Shea went around to the passenger side and got in. Looking

around the car she whistled at its elegant style. "This must have cost a fortune!"

"Like my dad can't afford it," Sylvie shrugged, pushing at the myriad of buttons arranged across the dashboard. "Look at all this stuff. This car does everything." She bounced around on the posh leather seats.

Shea looked across the panel reading the buttons. "It's even got a sun roof!"

Sylvie reached up and turned the knob opening the hatch. They both looked up into the clouds that were covering the moon. "Well, I guess we won't use this." She closed the roof again with a shiver.

Sylvie was a spoiled child who hid her high-spirited antics behind a buoyant head of chestnut hair and pouty lips pressed against a freckled face. Even the most enlightened being could not avoid falling prey to her piteous games. Always cheerful, Sylvie never let anyone get in the way of her happiness. She did whatever she damn well pleased, whenever she wanted to. Her parents were aware of the charms their daughter possessed. They tended to play along with the many tricks she was capable of using to get herself out of one jam or another. After all, they learned early on their little Sylvie had a knack for always landing right back on her feet. Sylvie dared people to rain on her parade. Often most wouldn't, but if you were arrogant enough to think you could mess with her, she had a monstrous temper she didn't hesitate to display.

Still, she made all her friends feel special when they were with her, like you were her only true friend in the whole world. According to Sylvie, friendship was the best thing ever invented. She kept a large network of friends in all aspects of her life. She believed you could never know too many people. Everyone had something to offer... after all, what are friends for if you can't use them? Yet Sylvie believed in true friendship and never really abused any of them.

Sylvie drove the car down the long, windy road, chatting about school and anything else that came to her mind. "Have you heard a word I've said?" she snapped suddenly.

Shea turned from the window she'd been aimlessly staring out. "What?"

"Where are you, Shea? I've been trying to have a conversation with you for the past twenty minutes."

Shea was thinking about her phone call with Billy. Readjusting her purse on her lap she stared out the window again. "Billy and I kind of had a tiff. He thinks I'm bored with him."

"Well, are you?"

"Of course not. I admit I'm not crazy about all the hours he's putting in, but I love him more than anything. I wonder where he came up with such a silly notion."

"College." Sylvie answered.

"Huh?" Shea faced her again.

"You're going off to college, right?"

"Yeah, but what does that have to do with it?"

"Billy's worried."

"About what?"

"Oh come on, Shea, it's so simple. You two have never been separated before. Now you're going off to school, you'll be two hours away from him, in dorms where there will be hundreds of men running around. He has a lot to be worried about."

"That's crazy. I don't want any of those guys."

"Billy doesn't know that. Not even you can say you won't meet someone new. I hate to say it, but it happens all the time."

"Then how can we have a relationship that's built on trust when he doesn't even think I'll come home? What am I supposed to do, not go to school?"

"All I'm saying is that's why he's acting strange. You can bet on it."

"I'll bring it up when I talk to him tomorrow."

"I wouldn't count out those college hunks so fast though, Shea. You might decide to change your mind."

"I doubt it, Sylvie. I wouldn't even know how to act around another man. Billy's all I've ever known."

"You're pathetic," giggled Sylvie.

Shea thought about what Sylvie had said. She couldn't see

herself with anyone but Billy. Just the thought of it made her shiver. Billy knew all her idiosyncrasies, she'd be terrified to even try accustoming herself to anyone other than him. She'd heard all the horror stories from her girlfriends who were out dating. She knew a long time ago she wanted no part of that circus.

Shea had to admit she was surprised Billy still excited her like he did. Whenever he walked into a room, Shea's heart would immediately start beating faster. She still got goose pimples when he touched her, and her knees grew weak when he kissed her. Just like it was the first time.

Sylvie flicked the radio dial and started singing. Shea turned to smile at her and noticed the speedometer. "Don't you think you're going a little bit fast, Sylvie?"

"I gotta see how much power this thing has. I can't go out in it if it handles like an old fogies' car." She ran her hand over the dash. "Man, this car does everything."

"Including crash," added Shea, sarcastically. "You're going to get a ticket if you're not careful."

"Oh, relax. There's not a cop for miles."

"Sylvie, we passed one at the last corner."

"Yeah, I know. But he didn't move." Sylvie looked in her rear view mirror, but ignored the headlights climbing on them. "Boy, this thing's got some power, huh?"

Shea didn't say a word, but watched in the side mirror as the car behind them moved closer. She checked the needle that was now hovering at the ninety mile an hour mark. Flashing lights suddenly reflected off the windows.

"Oops!" Sylvie quipped in a carefree tone. She pulled the car over to the shoulder and turned to see who was coming up alongside the car.

"I can't believe you got us stopped," snapped Shea.

Sylvie squinted into the mirror, trying to recognize the officer. Then she smiled. "Oh great, it's Greg. Piece of cake."

"He's a dirtbag," sniped, Shea.

"That may be, but he's easy. He'll never give me a ticket. He knows my father too well."

24

Shea nodded. Everyone knew Sylvie's dad. He was the top attorney in town. Shea had a profound respect for him because he was the lawyer who helped her out during her guardian case. She believed he was the only reason the judge voted in her favor. Their families had always been friendly. Shea's dad took care of the family's teeth for free, in return, Sylvie's dad helped Jim out during his crisis.

That was the way things worked in the little town they lived in and Shea loved it for the most part. Things did have a way of turning the tables though, and she despised the policeman, Greg, for that reason. He constantly asked her out, knowing full well she was involved with Billy. He used his power as an officer to try and intimidate her, saying he could give her tickets any time he pleased. He often stopped her just to harass her. He was liked by almost everyone because he rarely gave out tickets. Other girls who had been stopped, often accepted his request for a date in lieu of a ticket. Greg had his ass pretty well covered, so nothing Shea could ever say to incriminate him would be taken seriously.

Shea looked out her window, hoping Greg wouldn't see her. She hated any confrontation with him. His looks alone grossed her out which led her even more to believe when she saw a girl on his arm, it was repayment of a favor.

Sylvie rolled the window down and looked up at Greg. Shea wished at that moment she could evaporate. Greg leaned his tall scrawny body into the car, and smiled that goofy smile he was so famous for.

"Well hi, Miss Sylvie," he cooed in his fake southern accent. "This a new set of wheels we're sportin'?"

Sylvie smiled up at him. "Why yes, Gre... Officer Morrison. You like?" She held her hands out through the window like one of Bob Barker's girls on Price Is Right.

Greg stepped back, looking along the Mercedes' sleek body. "Pretty snazzy."

"You look really good, Greg. Have you done something different with your hair?" teased Sylvie.

Shea tried to suppress a laugh, but it escaped. Greg leaned in at

25

the noise. "Why Miss Shea, fancy meeting you here. Where you two headed?"

"We're going to the Ice House," answered Sylvie.

"I directed that question to Miss Shea."

Shea crossed her arms, turning away with a huff.

"What's the matter Shea, not in a visitin' mood tonight?" His tone was cutting.

"Greg, leave her alone."

"You were going pretty fast there. I could still give you a ticket, you know. Better tell your friend there to treat me a little nicer."

"If you want to give me a ticket go ahead, but leave her alone. I was the one driving."

"I'll let you go this time, but you should let your friend know she shouldn't be discourteous to officers of the law."

Shea couldn't hold her tongue any longer. She lashed out, spewing insults as fast as they could come to mind.

Sylvie quickly intervened, thanking Greg and closing the window before he could change his mind. She pressed on the gas, taking off so fast, stones spun up and hit the police car behind her.

Shea sensed her anger, but wouldn't back down on her outburst. Greg was a vile, pompous ass and he made her sear with fury.

"Nice move," Sylvie finally sputtered. "What are you trying to do, ruin my driving record?"

"Oh, right. You know he'd never give you a ticket. Not with your dad."

"Still, you could have been a little nicer to him. Shea, you better be careful, you never know when you're going to need him."

"I hope I never need him. He's about as incompetent as they come. He hides behind that badge of his. Take it away and he'd disintegrate into nothing."

"God, Shea. Why do you hate him so much?" Sylvie asked in a serious tone.

"Because he harasses me."

"He harasses all the girls in town. Ignore him like the rest of us."

Shea couldn't ignore the problems he gave her. She knew he picked on most of the girls in town, but he went much further when harassing her. Shea never told anyone about the time Greg stopped her just to ask her out. When she said no, he practically climbed in the car and raped her. If he hadn't received another call, Shea was sure he would have made good on his promise to '*teach her about respect,*' as he put it.

Shea looked back out the window, purposefully ignoring Sylvie. Her last comment really hurt. Why should anyone have to worry about ignoring some cad who's job it is to protect you in the first place?

◆　　◆　　◆

Shea looked at her watch again. It was getting near closing time and Sylvie had not yet come back. She'd gone to her friend Joyce's house to see her new baby sister. Shea stayed at the Ice House to talk to her friends as Sylvie had promised to only be a while.

It was really late. She looked around for signs of her friend, then went to the phone to call Joyce's house. They must have lost track of time, she thought, a little irritated. Joyce's mom answered the phone with a weary voice and told Shea they had left a few minutes before. She confirmed that Sylvie was aware she had to come back and pick up Shea.

"She hasn't forgotten you, Shea. Joyce is coming back with her. I guess they decided to go dancing, and Joyce will spend the night at Sylvie's. Anyway, they should be there any minute."

Shea hung up the phone, satisfied. She didn't want to go out dancing, but Sylvie could drop her off at home on the way. When she entered the pool hall area, she was surprised to see the place had almost cleared out. One guy offered her a ride home but she declined, settling into a booth to wait for Sylvie.

◆　　◆　　◆

"Damn!" Sylvie announced as the car came to a rolling stop.

The lights on the panel were all lit up. Perplexed, she looked at them, shaking her head. "I wonder what this means?" Slowly under her breath she studied the panels.

27

"What's wrong, Sylvie?" Joyce asked, confused.

"I don't know. Will you do me a favor and get the operator's manual out of the glove box?"

Joyce fumbled through the stack of papers while Sylvie tried to start the car again. It made a sputtering noise that almost caught but slowly died again.

"Sounds like the battery to me," Joyce said, gingerly searching for the book.

"Can't be." Sylvie tried to start it again. "The whole car is brand new. I'm reading the panels: looks like a problem with the car's computer."

"You're going to flood the engine if you keep doing that." Joyce handed over the manual, then carefully put the other contents back.

Sylvie reached over. Grabbing a flashlight she turned to the page with the instructions for the panel lights. It had been raining on and off all night, and now it was starting to come down again in buckets. The two girls looked through the windshield in despair.

"Shit," sighed Joyce.

"Don't worry. I think I have the problem solved." Sylvie made a few adjustments to the dashboard and tried to start the car again. Their hopes soared when it looked like it might turn over, but the engine coughed to silence. "Damn!" Sylvie said in frustration, slamming her hands against the steering wheel.

"What are we going to do?" demanded Joyce.

"We'll walk back to your house. I have to call the Ice House and let Shea know we're on our way."

Sylvie took the umbrella off the back seat and opened the door on her side. With a sigh she turned to Joyce. "Stay there. I'll come around to your side and get you. I can't believe my new shoes!" she wailed, stepping out into the downpour.

The two girls trudged up the hill back to Joyce's house, a good two miles away. The wind whipped the rain around in a fury as they huddled together under the umbrella and braced themselves against the torrent

Connie came out from the kitchen and noticed Shea sitting in the half-dark. Most of the lights had been shut off to signal the place was closed. "Shea, what's up?" she asked, approaching the table.

Shea leaned back against the wall and pulled her feet up on the seat in front of her.

"Sylvie was supposed to come and get me, I don't know where she is. I just called and they said she was on her way. I know you're closing up, sorry. I can wait outside."

Connie shrugged her off. "No need. I still have some work to do in back. Look, if she's not here by the time I finish, I can take you home."

Shea sighed with relief. "Thanks, I think they forgot me."

Connie waved and disappeared into the kitchen again.

Shea watched the rain fall against the window. She checked the head lights as they came up the road, hoping each time that it was Sylvie. She couldn't have forgotten, Joyce's mother had reassured her of that. She twirled the salt shaker around on the table and checked her watch. She was about to get up and call Joyce's house again when a car pulled into the lot. Jumping up, she ran to the door.

Her eyes popped when she saw her cousin Sarah open the door of the black pickup and fall out onto the walkway. Shea quickly pulled her cousin off the ground. "What on earth?"

Sarah scrambled to her feet and let out a giggle. Shea pulled her into the restaurant to sit her down. "What are you doing?"

"I'm drunk." Sarah laughed as she slid down the side of the cigarette machine.

"I can see that." Shea helped her into a chair. She turned and looked back out at the man waiting in the truck. "Who are you with?"

Sarah jumped up as if she'd just remembered the man in the truck. "Oops! I'm supposed to be using the potty."

Shea looked at him again. He gave her the creeps. "Who is he?" she insisted.

Sarah headed to the rest room with Shea in tow holding her up as she walked. "His name's Kevin. Ain't he a doll?"

That wasn't the term Shea had in mind, but pushing it aside she helped her cousin maneuver her clothing. Sarah closed the stall door leaving Shea outside.

"How do you know him?" continued Shea.

"I met him tonight." Sarah finally slurred after a long pause. Truth was Sarah didn't remember much of the evening, but she didn't like being interrogated. "God, who are you... my mother? He was at a party I went to." She flushed and made her way to the sink. He's really nice. We talked for hours."

Shea helped Sarah take her mascara out of her purse.

"He took me out dancing," added Sarah, loudly.

"You just met him tonight?" Shea commented.

Sarah nodded and looked through her purse for some gum.

"So, you just picked him up?"

"You make me sound cheap. We met at a party, which got boring and he asked if I wanted to go dancing. He's really nice, Shea, you'll see."

Shea just shook her head in disgust. "He took you out and got you drunk. You call that nice?"

"Oh yes! He made me drink all those drinks. I've been drinking since my party this afternoon. Come on, Shea! It's graduation night. Everyone's out drinking. Hell, I've been to three parties since I left mine." She paused. "By the way, what were you and my mom fighting about?"

Shea finished brushing her hair and put the brush back in Sarah's purse. "Oh, it was nothing."

"My mom can be impossible sometimes. It doesn't help when she's been drinking either. She gets so ornery. She was wasted when I left. She and her old friends were sitting in the dining room cracking up at nothing. Parents can be such geeks," Sarah rambled on, not paying attention to Shea's mood. "Besides, I'm not that drunk." She stepped back from the sink to show her cousin she could now stand. She swayed a little but managed to keep her footing.

30

"Well, be careful. It's not good to pick up strangers like that."
Sarah smirked and put her arm around her cousin. "With all
due respect Shea, sounds like my mother's rubbing off on you. I'm
a big girl, I can take care of myself." They walked out of the
restroom together, toward the front door. "By the way, what are
you doing here all by yourself?"

Shea shrugged. "Sylvie is supposed to be picking me up. I was
waiting for her when you pulled up. Hopefully, she'll be waiting for
me now." She made her way to the door and looked out beyond
Kevin's truck into the empty lot. "Seems strange she's still not
here."

"We'll bring you home," offered Sarah.

"That's okay, I can wait." Shea felt uncomfortable. "Sylvie
should be here any minute."

"Don't be ridiculous Shea, it's right on our way home. I insist.
Come on, I want you to meet Kevin anyway."

Shea thought for a moment. Sarah was right. It was obvious
Sylvie wasn't coming and it was on the way to Sarah's house. Still,
Kevin gave her the heebie-jeebies. But Shea decided if anything
was going to happen, she and Sarah both could beat this guy. She
didn't like the idea of getting in the truck with him, but she didn't
want her cousin with him either. Being as drunk as she was she
would have a hard time fighting off any attack. She decided to go
home with Sarah, if for nothing else to take care of her.

Sarah threw the truck door open and jumped into the seat next
to Kevin. "Kevin, this is my cousin, Shea. Can we give her a ride
home?" Tossing her hair back, she moved closer to Kevin to make
room for Shea.

Kevin shrugged. "Sure. Where are you going?"

"You can take me to Sarah's," Shea said reluctantly as she
climbed into the big cab.

"Don't be silly," giggled Sarah, "we'll take you to your house.
Kevin and I may still want to do something...."

"Don't you think you should be going home, Sarah?" asked
Kevin.

"You've had an awful lot to drink," added Shea.

Sarah turned to Kevin, whispering, "You'll have to excuse her. Shea's a bit dull."

Shea nudged her. "Stop!" she grumbled under her breath.

Kevin pulled out onto the highway, keeping one eye on his pretty ride. He thought Sarah was nice looking, but her cousin was far nicer. He couldn't help but notice her large breasts. "I tend to agree with your cousin, Sarah. Maybe I ought to get you home." He smiled at Shea.

Shea felt him staring, but didn't look back. She tried to ignore the fact his eyes were piercing a hole in her self confidence.

They rode along and talked. Kevin asked where they had gone to school and Sarah mentioned Shea was going out with Billy. She did this mostly to let Kevin know she wasn't available. She couldn't help but notice the attention Shea had attracted from Kevin. This wasn't uncommon at all. Shea attracted attention wherever she went, Sarah might even have felt a hint of jealousy if she didn't know how hopelessly in love Shea and Billy were. All Sarah usually had to do, was tell the unsuspecting dude about Billy, then she could bask in the attention again. Sarah brought up the subject of Billy again. She seemed relieved that Kevin seemed to take an interest in the relationship. He asked all kinds of questions.

Kevin offered Cokes to the girls, taking one for himself. He nonchalantly took the pill he had been holding and dumped it into the can Sarah was holding. Shea hadn't taken one for herself, but took a sip from Sarah's when she offered. As they drove through the dark, Shea felt herself becoming light-headed and woozy. The clouds seemed to pass over the moon at an alarming rate. She had to prop her elbow up on the armrest to hold her head up. She looked over at Sarah whose head was bobbing up and down. It only took her a second to realize what was happening.

"Sarah, wake up," she pleaded, shaking her violently. "What did you do to her?" Her tone was terse. "Stop the truck... let us out!" She reached over past Sarah and grabbed Kevin. "I said *stop!*"

Kevin slammed on the brakes in the middle of the road and threw the truck in park. "Okay," he said calmly.

Shea tried to blast him again. Feeling herself getting dizzy, she took hold of the dashboard for support and threw open the door. Sliding off the seat, she almost fell when her feet finally hit the ground. When she turned around Kevin was behind her. She turned back to get Sarah but Kevin caught her. "Don't worry about her. She'll sleep for a while."

"Get away from me, you slime!" Shea pushed him away. "Sarah!" Kevin tore her away from the truck. Shea kicked at him but lost her footing. As Kevin reached out to catch her she kicked her leg with all her might, landing her booted foot deep into his groin. He stumbled backwards and let out a curse.

Shea took off. Screaming, she ran through the open field into the night. There were houses off in the distance and she tried to run as fast as she could to get to them. She no longer thought about getting Sarah. She had to save herself.

As she ran, her purse waved behind her. Adrenaline took over, dispelling the dizzy spells. She didn't look behind her. All she could think about is getting help.

The ground was wet and very soft, it was like running through honey. Shea knew it slowed her but she ran like she never had before. She pleaded with her body, coaxing her legs into action.

She heard Kevin behind her and willed her feet to move faster. Suddenly something grabbed her purse. Instinctively she let it go, not breaking the swift motion of her body. She chanced a glance behind her to see how close he was when he got hold of her. Shea's foot hit something and she tumbled forward. She struggled to get back up but tripped again. The brutal power of Kevin's body forced her to the ground. Her head snapped forward, hitting something hard. She tried to fight but the energy left her. She was no match to his enormous stature. He pinned her to the ground. Head spinning, she felt herself tumbling into a pool of darkness, then everything went black.

◆   ◆   ◆

The storms had passed and the night air was finally clear. A group of high school boys tromped through the moonlit field toward their special hiding place in the woods. No grown-ups, not even the cops, knew about the teens' place. It was a well known party scene, and most of the kids met there on the weekends. Someone would get a keg and build a bonfire. With the weather finally cleared, the boys were making their way to the party spot to see if anyone was there. If not, they bought their own liquor and were prepared to party by themselves.

The boys teased each other, laughing on the way to the woods. They had already been drinking in the car. That was the next most common thing to do if the weather was foul.

Scurrying along the wet hay, it was Tim who noticed it first. He'd tripped on something and when he looked down he was surprised to see a purse. They opened it to find an I.D., but couldn't see the writing in the dark. They didn't pay much attention to it, thinking it must belong to someone at the party place.

A few more feet along, they tripped over Shea. Tim jumped back, screaming, "A body! It's a body!" He ran away in shock. The other boys dashed up and checked it out.

Mark being a volunteer EMT, put his finger to her neck. Most of the boys in that rural area were volunteer firemen or EMT's. It was common out there where they didn't have paid fire and emergency personnel. "She's got a pulse. Someone run back and get the car." He checked the girl's injuries while one of the other boys took off toward the car. "She's got some head injuries." He continued to check the cuts on her face. "Someone help me lift her. We'll have to carry her out a ways. The car will never make it through all this mud."

The other two boys with Tim helped to carry her. They were met halfway with the car. Quickly, they put her in the back seat and rushed to the hospital. They had already been drinking and were a little afraid of being caught driving drunk, but they knew they had to help. Still, they didn't want to get in trouble, so after they checked her in, they slipped quietly out of the waiting room and left.

◆　　　◆　　　◆

Shea groggily awoke to a green room with white cupboards on the wall. She pulled herself up. Looking down at herself she gasped. Her clothes had been removed and she was wearing a light checkered cotton gown.

At first she didn't remember anything, but slowly her mind focused on the terrible events that had taken place earlier. Tears slowly started brimming around her eyes. She remembered running through the field away from her attacker, then falling, but everything went blank after that. Then as if she suddenly remembered something, she put her fingers to her head and confirmed what she already she knew.

Shea turned when she saw a nurse appear from around the curtain. "Oh finally," beamed the nurse. "We were beginning to worry about you."

Shea stared blankly at her. She was a pretty woman, her skin a smooth tawny color. Her hair was pulled back in a bun and glowed with luster. Her eyes were very generous and she spoke with a soft calming voice. "Are you feeling better? That was quite a fall you took."

"Where am I?" Shea finally asked.

The nurse took Shea's wrist and studied her watch for a moment. Putting Shea's hand back down by her side, she answered, "You're in the emergency room."

"Yes I know, but what hospital... how did I get here?" Shea tried to sit up but the pain in her head caused her to get dizzy. The nurse raised the bed so she was in a sitting up position.

"You're at Albany Med and your friends brought you in. But they left in an awful hurry." She paused for a moment, fixing the blanket over Shea again. "I have my suspicions they were drunk. How much have you had?"

Shea shook her head. "I don't know what you're talking about. I wasn't with anyone and I certainly wasn't drinking."

The nurse looked at her in surprise. She expected that Shea would lie to protect herself from her parents, but something told her she was telling the truth. She sat down on the bed next to her.

"Why don't you tell me what happened?"

Shea remembered what she could. As the story slowly unfolded, Shea couldn't stop the tears that stung her eyes. She continued, telling the nurse about riding with her cousin and Kevin, and how he drugged both of them. By the time she finished her account of the story, she was sobbing. The nurse held her hand to calm her before excusing herself.

A few minutes later she returned with the doctor. "Shea, this is Dr. Alder. Considering what you told me we think we should do an internal exam. I hate to say this but chances are you were raped."

Shea sat dumbfounded, letting the nurse's words absorb. She held her palm to her face. How could this be happening? "Sarah." she said quietly. "My cousin Sarah was in the car too. What happened to her?"

The nurse shook her head. "Honey, you're the only one they brought in here. I don't know what happened to your cousin."

The doctor had the receptionist call the police. "Will you be willing to make a statement?" he asked. Shea nodded.

"This may be a little painful," explained the nurse, "but we need these tests for the police report."

Shea didn't say anything, but her eyes let the nurse know she understood.

"Oh, I called your guardian," the nurse added, taking Shea's hand. "I found the number in your wallet."

"Where was that?"

"In your purse. It was with you when you came in."

Shea realized that whoever had dropped her off must have found her purse too. She was grateful to them. "Can I have it?" she asked.

"Sure, I'll get it when we finish here. It's in the bag with the rest of your things."

Shea was relieved when the doctor said he was through. It wasn't as painful as she'd thought it was going to be. He also took pictures, which made Shea feel miserable and embarrassed. She wished she could pull the covers up over her head. The exam was intrusive enough, without pictures for the police report.

The nurse got her bag from the corner of the room and handed it to her. Shea looked through her things, examining the damage. Every inch of her clothes were covered in mud. Locating her wallet, she checked the contents. Everything was still there, the I.D. card placed back where the nurse had gotten it.

Shea was still in a daze when the doctor came back and told her a police officer waited in the other room to ask her questions.

"Are you ready for this, Miss Parks?" inquired the nurse.

Shea was very ready. This monster had put her through enough. She wanted him caught. Bracing herself, she told the doctor to let the officer in. She quickly tucked the blanket in around her to cover herself from the officer she knew might possibly verbally attack her. She'd seen before how these rape things work. She would be interrogated and accused. It never worked the other way, but she knew she had to make a report. If she didn't it was considered an admission of guilt.

She realized how true her thoughts were when she saw Greg trot into the room. All hope she did have disappeared at the sight of him. She could tell he was as surprised to see her too. He pulled a note pad from his jacket pocket, then searched the other ones for a pen.

"Well, Miss Shea. We meet again. Good thing for you I worked overtime. Who knows what would have happened if I hadn't been here."

Shea shuddered. "If you can't do your job professionally, I can arrange to have another officer come here. One who knows how to do his job."

"I know my job perfectly. I'm not here to give you a hard time, I just want to help you. Besides it's busy tonight and I'm the only one available."

Shea was surprised at his gentle tone. She relaxed a little and listened to the questions. The doctor came back in the room to confirm there had been penetration. Shea shriveled up inside when she heard the word.

She relayed the story to Greg as best as she could remember. She told him Sarah was with her, and that they had both been drugged. She was still worried about Sarah, wondering what had happened to her.

She didn't wonder long; a few moments later Sarah and her

mother bounded into the room. Shea almost leapt off the gurney when she saw her cousin standing there as if nothing had happened. "Sarah?"

"Shea, what happened to you?"

Dumbfounded, Shea stared at Sarah. "You're all right."

Her cousin looked at her strangely. "Why shouldn't I be? What happened?"

Shea shook her head. Here was her cousin standing in front of her with nothing but a look of confusion on her face. Not a hair was out of place and she was dressed in the outfit she wore that night. "Why shouldn't I be?" Shea repeated in disbelief. "Sarah, do you remember anything about last night?"

Sarah shook her head. "I remember drinking a lot." She still felt out of sorts but figured it was the effects of the alcohol. "But I don't remember doing anything out of the ordinary."

"No," Shea retorted, "I mean about the ride home."

Sarah shook her head again. "Not much. Kevin woke me up when we got home. Why Shea, what happened?"

Shea leaned forward and wept. She tried to speak but nothing would come out.

Greg looked at her, perplexed. He tried to piece Shea's story together, but it seemed strange Sarah was there and didn't see or hear a thing. "Shea claims she was attacked by a man named Kevin. Apparently you were both in the truck," he said.

Sarah nodded in agreement. "Yes, we were giving Shea a ride home. I fell asleep but Kevin woke me when we got to my house. We had already dropped Shea off."

Shea shook her head violently. "No, no," she cried. "He didn't take me home. Sarah, he drugged both of us. You fell into a drug induced sleep...."

"That's silly, Shea. Kevin told me he dropped you off at home."

"Sarah, we had already decided to go to your house. Why would I tell him to take me to mine?

"I don't know. Kevin said you wanted to go home so that's where he took you."

Caroline interrupted to get a better perspective on what was happening. "Shea, what is it you're trying to say?"

Shea shook with despair. "I was *raped*, Aunt Caroline. Kevin raped me and then left me in the woods to die."

Caroline raised a questioning eyebrow at the doctor. He nodded that something had taken place.

"Sarah, what time did you get home?" Shea asked sharply.

Sarah shrugged her shoulders. "I don't remember exactly. Around midnight maybe."

Shea rolled her eyes and wiped the tears that now fell from them. "You can't remember *anything!*"

The whole night was turning into a nightmare. Shea began to realize how ridiculous her story was starting to sound to everyone. She sat back, feeling hopeless. Who would ever believe her now with Sarah standing in front of her patronizing her every word, making it sound like she made the whole thing up? Shea was crushed. No one but she and her attacker saw anything. Shea wasn't even sure what really took place after she blacked out.

"I was drunk," offered Sarah. "I don't remember much of anything about last night. All I know is, Kevin brought me home safe and sound. I don't know what happened to you, but Kevin hardly seems the type of guy capable of doing such a thing."

The doctor was conversing with Caroline about the results of the exam. He collaborated with Shea that there had been sexual intercourse. He felt that by the looks of her something very terrifying had happened.

Greg finished taking both Shea's and Sarah's account of that evening's events. He made a few more notes, then excused himself.

"Oh, honestly Shea! I don't know how you get yourself into these messes," Caroline said when they were finally alone. "And how could Kevin have done such a thing to you and not Sarah?"

Shea could do nothing but cry. She didn't have the answers. She wouldn't want anyone to go through what she had, but it would have made her story more believable if Sarah had been a victim too. She also knew her aunt would turn the whole mess around to look like her fault. She was defeated. She had done all she could do to make her story known, all she could do now is hope the police would take her seriously enough to help her.

The ride home was pure hell. Shea felt as though she had been raped again. Her aunt and cousin did nothing to ease her fears. They threw a myriad of questions at her, none of which she could answer. She had been knocked cold and couldn't remember a thing.

"Then how do you know it was Kevin that raped you? Couldn't it have been one of the boys that brought you to the hospital?"

"It was Kevin that chased me! It was Kevin that drugged me, drugged *you*."

"I want to believe you, Shea, I really do, but I just don't think Kevin would do such a terrible thing."

"Why was he chasing me?"

"I don't know. Maybe he didn't want you to take off alone in the dark. Maybe, just maybe he was trying to bring you back to the truck. I'll tell you what, Shea. Kevin said he'd call me tomorrow. I'll ask him what went on."

"Oh, like he's ever going to show his face to you after this."

Sarah just glared at her with frustrated disbelief. "For your information he said he would call me tomorrow."

Shea stared silently out of the window the rest of the way home. She knew her words fell on deaf ears. No one believed her or cared what that monster had done to her.

"I want to go home, Aunt Caroline," she announced.

Caroline glanced at her in the rear view mirror. "The doctor said you should be watched for the next couple of days. That knot on your head looks pretty scary, you could have a slight concussion."

"Please, Aunt Caroline. I don't have any clothes with me and I'd like to take a shower."

"Really Shea, you should stay where you can be watched. I don't like the idea of you being in that house, all alone. What if something were to happen?"

Lee Ann's family had gone the ocean for her graduation. Shea had declined the invitation because she needed to pack for college.

She was due to leave next week, Lee Ann would be home just in time to say good-bye to her friend. Everything was packed. All Shea had left were the clothes she wore on a daily basis. She'd thought it prudent to get there early enough to find a part-time job and a decent place to live. Her thoughts returned to the car.

"Aunt Caroline, please! I promise I'll call you first thing this morning. I'd just feel better if I could sleep in my own bed."

"Oh, all right. But this is against my better judgment. Make sure you call me," sniffed Caroline.

"I promise." Shea felt a little more alive.

Her legs wobbled beneath her as she got out of the car. The pain was beginning to set in and she could feel the heat coming off the bump on her head. Saying her good-byes, she slowly walked to the house. When she got to her room she sat on the bed, crying her eyes out. She wondered how things had gotten so out of hand. Even the doctor hadn't believed she had been raped until he after his internal exam. Now after all was said and done, she had the burden of proving it actually happened. It was humiliating telling the officer that she'd gotten in the car with a stranger. Then how she was attacked next to the truck with her cousin sleeping inside, screaming for help with no one hearing. And almost worst of all was her aunt and cousin looking at her like she had made the entire thing up. Looking back over the facts she realized how crazy the whole thing sounded. Crazy but true.

Shea felt defeated. She didn't know what to do. Should she call Billy? But what would she tell him? She thought long and hard, then finally got up and went into the bathroom. Starting the shower she went to find something to put on. The hot shower felt good running over her as she felt herself calming for the first time since she'd gotten in the truck. Why hadn't she trusted her instincts? If only she had waited for Sylvie to return.

A sudden impulse to run away struck her. She tried to dismiss it, but the impulse persisted. Maybe it was the way. After all, she could come back when she wanted. An inkling of hope rose in her. Finishing her shower she quickly got dressed.

Florida was her only hope now. Knowing the story of her rape

41

claim would soon be all over this small town, she couldn't bear to face the unending line of questions and speculation. Of course she'd never be able to defend herself against them. No, that's not how things worked in that town. They'd all gossip and speculate about what happened, but no one would ever seek the truth. Now she was convinced she had to leave. If not to save herself, then to save Billy from the embarrassment.

Billy! she groaned. What will I tell him? She forced herself not to brood on it for long, she needed to get out of here as soon as possible. She knew that by leaving she had as good as admitted she was wrong, but she didn't care. That monster Kevin was still out there; she couldn't face seeing him again. She could call Billy from her aunt's house in Florida and explain everything. She needed time to get over it, he would understand.

The sun was just peaking over the horizon when Shea finally finished loading the car. She wanted to get out before anyone woke up and saw her.

She scribbled a quick note to Lee Ann and her family telling them good-bye and thanking them for the past year. *I'll be in touch*, she wrote, leaving the note on the table.

◆　　　◆　　　◆

She knew the place to go was Aunt Vicki's. She would understand Shea's plight, and right now Shea didn't know where else to turn. Vicki would help make sense of it all. Yes! Of anyone, Aunt Vicki would know what to do and what to say. Shea would only stay for a couple of weeks then she'd be able to come back home with a renewed sense of what to do. She just needed to get where someone would comfort her, and tell her everything was all right.

Tears stung Shea's eyes as drove to the Thruway. She knew Billy would be hurt, but in the end he'd understand. She had to get away from Aunt Caroline. She'd said so many damaging things over the past few days. Probably mad because in two weeks when Shea left for college, Caroline would no longer have her under her thumb. Her aunt was obsessed with controlling every situation. Shea knew it had upset her greatly when the courts allowed Shea to live with the Lee Ann instead of her. She displayed so much control over her own family it was clear even if Sarah agreed with Shea on anything, Caroline would ultimately harass her into changing her mind. It had always been that way. Every time Sarah tried to assert her opinion, mom would step in and badger until she gave up and agreed with her just to shut her up.

The most important question that remained was what Shea would tell Billy. She didn't want him chasing her to Florida. She wanted this time to get herself together. She comforted herself with the thought that she would call him when she got to Aunt Vicki's.

As she drove away from her hometown, the sun was high. The heat and humidity were already starting to bear down on her head. She put on a baseball cap and sunglasses to hide the ugly bruises. Already her mind was starting to clear. The fact she would see Aunt Vicki made her feel she was doing the right thing.

$\mathscr{C}$HAPTER FOUR

Sarah sat at the breakfast bar with her toast and coffee, trying to read the morning paper. It was already ten o'clock and she was still feeling the effects of a massive hangover. Pulling her white silk robe closed, she thought about the scene in the hospital earlier that morning. She truly wished she hadn't fallen asleep. She knew she was pretty drunk, but for Kevin to drug her? She kept on going over the events in her head again and again. It still didn't make any sense. She just couldn't believe Kevin could be responsible for such an ugly act as rape.

Her mother entered the kitchen and headed for the coffee maker. The sun was finally showing after two days of rain and the birds were flying around the feeder that sat outside the kitchen window.

"Isn't it pretty out this morning?" she asked Sarah.

Sarah looked up from the paper. "Yes," she replied half heartily. "Mom, who was that on the phone earlier?"

Caroline turned from the window and went to the table for some sugar. "It was Shea."

"How is she?"

Caroline gave a slight shrug. "She sounded fine. Said she was calling in like she promised, felt good and would be out most of the day."

Sarah sighed. "That sure was a strange night. What do you suppose happened?"

Caroline went to the other side of the table to open the sliding glass door before sitting down. "I really don't know. The nurse pulled me aside and told me some boys brought her in."

Sarah stared into space for a moment. "What boys?"

"I don't know, honey. The whole story sounds crazy. Maybe after she got home some friends stopped over to pick her up."

Sarah shook her head. "That just doesn't sound like Shea. I've never seen her go out with anyone but Billy."

"Your cousin can do some pretty crazy things. Just the fact she'd give up living in a house like this, so she could finish school with her friends."

"I can't blame her for that," muttered Sarah. "I think I'd feel the same way."

"Well honey, that's different. You have better friends than Shea. I mean, what kind of friend would leave her stranded somewhere?"

Sarah knew she was talking about Sylvie leaving Shea stranded at the Icehouse the night before. She was friends with Sylvie too, and was surprised at her thoughtlessness.

"Sylvie's my friend too," she announced.

"Yes, but you know how irresponsible she is, and you wouldn't let yourself get in the same situation. Plus, you know you could call your father or me and we'd pick you up. We would have picked Shea up too. I'm sorry, I know you like your cousin, but she does lack common sense. She's just like her father that way."

Sarah rolled her eyes and went back to reading the paper.

Caroline looked out into the back yard and thought about the work that needed to be done. "I think I'm going to give you that one plot down there in the back, see what you can do with it. You need something to keep you busy this summer, anyway."

Sarah looked out the window too. "What are you talking about?"

Caroline pointed to the small plot of weeds near the back of the yard. "You know, where the vegetable garden used to be. Why don't you get some flowers and fill it in?"

Sarah had made the mistake of telling her mom she needed a project for the summer and was interested in gardening. She had watched Caroline transform the sides of the house into flowering pictures. Her mom definitely had a green thumb, some of her work was even featured in a local gardening magazine.

Sarah was saved from replying as the phone rang. Running excitedly to answer it, she figured it was probably Kevin calling like he said he would. Her heart rose as she picked up the receiver, but

45

quickly sank when she heard the voice at the other end. "Oh, hi Billy. No, Shea isn't here, just a minute. Mom! Where was Shea when she called?"

Caroline came back in from the patio. "I think she was home. Why?"

"It's Billy. He's wondering where she is."

Caroline made her way across the kitchen and took the phone from Sarah. "Hi, Billy. Shea said she had some last minute errands to run before she left next week. Yes, well I'm sure you're in her travel plans today. She'll probably stop by. I wouldn't worry. Oh, no problem. You have a nice day. Bye."

"That's strange," commented Sarah. "Shea and Billy always talk to each other before they do anything for the day." She cleared her cup and plate from the bar and folded the paper back up. "Shea said something to me last night at the Icehouse. She said she and Billy had a fight on the phone."

The doorbell rang and Caroline left the room to answer it. "Well, I wouldn't worry about those two," she called, "they'll work it out." She looked down at her watch. It was ten o'clock and she wasn't expecting anyone. "I wonder who that could be?" Opening the door she was pushed back by an enormous bouquet of red roses. "Whoa... what's this?"

The flower man looked down at his clipboard. "I have a delivery for a Sarah."

"That's my daughter." Caroline took the clipboard to sign.

"Line five." He handed her the pen.

She quickly scrawled her name, thanked the young man and carried the flowers to the kitchen. "Sarah?"

Sarah came back in from the porch and looked in surprise at the huge bouquet. "Who are they for?"

"You. Here, quick." She handed them to her. "Who are they from?"

Sarah took the card from the holder and slit the top open with her fingernail. *'Dear Sarah, thank you for a wonderful evening, I really had a nice time. I'll be out of town for a few days but would like to have dinner with you when I get back. I'll call you then. Love always, Kevin.'*

46

Sarah held the card close to her heart as she danced around the room. "I can't believe it, Mom. Did you hear that? *'Love* Kevin!'" Caroline smiled as she sniffed one of the buds. "These are pretty expensive, my dear. What does your friend do for a living?" Sarah grabbed her mom's arm. "Get this, Mom... he owns his own businesses. That's plural, as in more than one." She folded the huge bunch in her arms. "I can't even get my arms around these.

"I think he likes you," smiled Caroline, striding from the room.

Sarah gazed longingly at her roses, counting the buds one at a time. "Twenty-four," she said to herself excitedly, hardly able to contain herself. Thrusting her doubts of the night before aside, she concentrated on the tall dark stranger who had made her feel she was the only woman that existed. She remembered sitting at the table at the disco talking to him about everything, even her hopes and dreams. He shared his thoughts on his businesses and life. It was all so perfect, so mature. That was what she liked most about him, his maturity. She didn't dare tell her mom how old he was. She'd introduce them first so Caroline could see how wonderful Kevin was, then his age wouldn't matter.

Taking the flowers to the dining room, she set them in the middle of the table. She had first thought about putting them in her room, but she wanted everyone to see them. Finally she had a significant other. Just like Shea, only better. She could only bet Billy never gave Shea flowers. Not like these anyway. She bent to smell a bud, then dreamily walked to her room to get dressed.

♦   ♦   ♦

Kevin sat in the big leather chair watching the woman across the wooden desk. She pored over the papers in front of her, nodding and highlighting portions of the application.

"Mr. Kendall," she spoke at last, "it's so nice to finally meet you. My husband and I are sorry to hear your dad's not well, but everyone must retire sometime."

Kevin acknowledged her sympathies and continued. "Then you'll consider my proposal?"

She looked up from the papers again. "We have worked with your

47

father for a long time, Mr. Kendall. I have to say it's highly unlikely he would ask for credit. He didn't believe in it. He always paid cash for everything."

Kevin got up, pacing back and forth in front of the desk. "Yes, I know all that, and don't think my dad and I won't discuss it. See, Ms. Finley, the garden center has been booming, and Dad...." He paused a moment. "Well, Dad has been too ill to do much more than what was necessary, but my brothers and I feel it's time to expand again. Now, don't worry about Dad. We'll talk to him. I just need your approval to get started." He turned to face her. "What do you say?"

Fran sat back in her chair. "He's always been a great customer. I can't see any reason for denying it." She leaned forward and signed the application in front of her. Then she rose, reaching out to shake Kevin's hand.

"Hot dog!" shouted Kevin. "Now, you gotta promise me something, Ms. Finley."

"Okay." She nodded her head.

"Not a word about this to my father." He took a card from his front pocket. "As a matter of fact, if you have any questions, please call me at this number." His voice went to a whisper. "We gotta break Dad into this idea slowly. I know he'll agree to it once he sees it'll work, but we have to go slow. You understand?" He gave her hand one final squeeze.

Nodding her understanding. Fran smiled to herself as she sat back down. She was excited to close such a big deal. Profits had been slipping and with this big a sale, even if it was on credit, she knew it was a big boost to their profits. She knew Jake was good as his word.

CHAPTER FIVE

Shea pulled in the driveway almost to the front door. Jumping out, she pounded on the bell. She waited outside the big oak doors for what seemed to be forever. When the door finally swung open, she flew into her aunt's arms, almost toppling them both over.

Shea had contacted Aunt Vicki after she left New York. Vicki seemed surprised to hear she was driving down, but detected from their conversation Shea was determined to get away for some reason she wouldn't explain on the phone. From the tone of Shea's voice, she knew it was serious. Shea didn't tell her much, but said something bad had happened and she needed to come and stay with her for a while. Vicki was concerned about her driving all that way alone, so they set up a time she would be off the road each evening when Shea would call from her hotel room. She'd even wired her money, since Shea couldn't get access to her bank accounts right away.

Shea finally let Aunt Vicki go. "Thank God, I'm here at last!" She slumped tiredly, moving into the foyer.

Her aunt followed, taking in the bumps and lesions pasted across Shea's forehead and cheeks. "You look good, except for that nasty knot on your head," she observed. "What happened?"

Shea stalled for a moment before she told her aunt the story. Aunt Vicki was surprised at Shea's calmness at first. As a nurse she understood the devastation rape could have on a person. She surmised the only reason Shea had made it to Florida at all was she was in shock. This was common to see in any victim of a violent crime. Adrenaline takes over and makes the person do incredible things. As the details began to unravel, Vicki became angry. If she didn't know her sister Caroline so darn well, she wouldn't have believed anyone could have been so callous.

When Shea finally finished, Vicki comforted her sobbing niece in her arms until the tears stopped. She held back the rage that was building up inside her. For the moment her priority was to see if Shea was all right. "Did the doctor do a pelvic exam?" she questioned, still wondering how it happened. She knew Shea was responsible enough to keep herself safe and from what she knew she was still seeing Billy.

"Yes," Shea hung her head in misery. Vicki helped her sit down and explain everything she could remember about that night. Her voice became ragged as she described what took place in the emergency room. She could tell that Vicki was as angry as she was over the incident, but she just sat quietly listening. Shea was glad she didn't ask all kinds of questions. After the interrogation she encountered in the emergency room, all she wanted was for someone to hear her side of the story and believe her. It was one of the many qualities Shea appreciated about her aunt. She was always willing to listen without passing judgment or asking unanswerable questions.

After a while Shea calmed down and Vicki showed her to her room. She helped her carry her luggage up the stairs and went in to open the curtains for her niece. Shea still had a stiffness in her walk.

"The shock must be wearing off," she offered as Shea limped into the room.

"Yeah, all of a sudden, too. I didn't feel like this on the way down here." Shea winced as she put the bag she was carrying on the bed.

"It's normal," Vicki explained, "you must be tired." Shea nodded quietly. "Why don't you take a nap? I've got some things to do downstairs, anyway." One of which was to call her sister and let her have it for allowing Shea to end up in this situation in the first place. She was seething inside, but hid it as best she could so she wouldn't upset Shea. Vicki pulled the bed covers down and fluffed the pillow before excusing herself.

Shea settled uncomfortably onto the side of the bed and bent slowly to take off her shoes. The stiffness made it hard for her to move. She rolled slowly onto the bed and pulled the covers up over her. With the temperature being downright hot outside, Vicki kept the air almost frigid in the house. It wasn't long before Shea drifted off into an uneasy slumber. Her dreams carried her back to that horrible night she'd been trying to forget, but she couldn't seem to wake herself from the terrifying images. Her body was exhausted but her mind was still totally aware of the angry, helpless feelings that consumed her. It was like a horrible monster that wouldn't let go.

Shea tossed and turned for a long time before she finally sat up. Her aunt was talking to someone on the phone. She sounded downright upset because she was yelling and cursing like she'd never heard her do before. Shea listened for a moment.

Vicki stood with the receiver pressed against her ear. She wiped away the tears and recounted the details of Shea's horrifying ordeal. As she talked about it, her anger rose. Her sister's behavior had been deplorable. Now she let Caroline know just how she felt about her inexcusable attitude during it all.

She knew her sister to be cold and callous, but this unnerved her. How could she have been this despicable toward Shea? This was not going to be the end of it. So many times the past few days she wanted to call Caroline and tell her Shea was on her way to Florida and was fine. She thought for sure Caroline would be truly worried, but Shea made her promise she wouldn't call her until she got there. Now she knew why.

Vicki let out a good belt of reprimand to her sister. "How can you even think Shea could be capable of making up such a serious lie? Caroline, you take the cake. If there was any way I could have you arrested for what happened to her, believe me, I would. Shea will be staying with me. I will trust you will get all her paperwork sent to me at once."

"Now Vicki, don't go spouting off. I can understand how Shea feels, really! I don't doubt something happened either. I just feel Shea blew things all out of proportion. After all it was a group of boys that brought her into the emergency room in the first place." She emphasized the words. "They had all been drinking. Things just got out of hand. I think you ought...."

"Ought nothing, Caroline. Shea didn't even know those boys. She doesn't need to be around people who don't believe her and won't help her. I'll take care of things from here on. If I don't have those papers by the beginning of next week, you'll be hearing from my lawyer. Is that understood?"

"Whatever, Vicki." Caroline's tone was cool. "She was fool headed enough to drive herself down there and she is seventeen. If she wants to stay there I suppose there's nothing I can do about it anyway."

Vicki slammed the receiver back down in the cradle. Twirling around on her heel, she went into the kitchen. She jumped when she looked up and saw Shea standing on the landing. Shea made her way down the stairs and joined her. She knew from what her aunt had been saying that Caroline still believed it was the boys who did this to her, and that it wasn't really rape. All she could do when she thought about it was cry. Was Vicki the only one who believed her? It horrified her to think of the rumors going around town. Eventually Billy would hear. Would he think she was lying too? She had to write to him. She would sit down tonight and write him a long letter explaining everything. Whatever she did she couldn't bring herself to call him. She just couldn't face talking to anyone, the questions would be too much for her to handle right now. She would tell Billy everything, stressing the fact that she needed time to sort things out. Having made that decision, she felt better, although she still couldn't seem to stop crying.

Vicki took her sobbing niece in her arms. "Shea," Aunt Vicki is here. I believe you, dear. We will take care of this together. Do you hear me, sweetie?" She pulled Shea back so she could look at her. "We will get the criminal who did this to you."

Shea wasn't sure if it was the shock wearing off or the fact she felt safe but she felt free for the first time since the attack. It was like she couldn't allow herself to get emotional until she was safe. Vicki always made everything all right.

"So, Aunt Caroline told you the same story she heard from the hospital," sighed Shea between sniffles.

Vicki nodded. "Just because they brought you in doesn't make them guilty. You've told me who it was, now we just have to find him."

"Good luck. Do you really think he'll show his face again after what he did?"

Vicki shook her head. "Probably not, but maybe Sarah can give us the information we need."

Shea put her hand up to stop her aunt. "I don't want to talk to either of them. Sarah won't do anything but lie anyway. She already told me she doesn't believe me and that Kevin wasn't capable of doing such a thing. And if he was, why didn't he rape both of us?"

"You said you made a police report, right?" Shea nodded. "Well, then first thing tomorrow we'll call and get that... and the hospital report too." Vicki was still seething over her phone call with Caroline. She understood fully what Shea was up against now. She would have to do this by herself.

She knew she wouldn't have Caroline's help.

◆   ◆   ◆

The next morning, Vicki called information and got the number for the local police in New Salem. It was then that she learned there was no police report made that night.

"It was on June 26th. The report was taken at Albany Med," she repeated to the officer on the other end.

Shea came down the stairs quietly. She stood on the bottom step, listening. Her heart sank for the second time, yet somehow she wasn't surprised either. The police report was missing. What a fitting end to her horrible nightmare. This whole rape thing was a bad dream that wouldn't stop. Now, every piece of evidence had disappeared. The only thing left to remind her it was a nasty bump on her head and pain inside of her that told her she had been violated in the worst way. She didn't have the strength to fight anymore. She had no idea a rape could do all this to a person. A man attacked her, yet she felt she was the guilty one. All eyes and fingers pointed to her. What had she done that was so wrong, besides trusting the wrong person?

Vicki stopped when she saw Shea standing in the doorway. She

53

quickly put the receiver down and went to her. "Did you sleep well?"

Shea came into the room and sat down. "Okay, I guess. I haven't been able to sleep much since that night. Now I know why women don't report rapes," she commented sadly.

Vicki knew then, Shea had heard the conversation. She sat down next to Shea and put her arm around her. "I'm sorry."

"I'm not surprised. When the officer came in to interview me it was awful. He asked me all kinds of questions like I was the one responsible for what happened. He asked me personal things about my sexual behavior. I believe his exact word was 'prowess'." Shea pulled her sweater tightly around her and crossed her arms in front of her. "It was like being raped all over again, it was horrible. I've thought about nothing else all the way down here, Aunt Vicki. I don't want to do anything... there's no way of finding this guy and even if there was, it's his word against mine. Sarah was in the truck and heard nothing. I can't do this anymore, it's like reliving the whole thing over again and again." She broke down. "I've been made out to be the bad guy. I want to forget it Aunt Vicki. I need to get on with my life. I know I may be in denial right now, but I can't keep reliving this thing! I came here to clear my head and put myself back together, as far away from that place as possible." Tears streamed down her cheeks. "Please don't bring it here, Aunt Vicki."

Vicki took Shea in her arms. "I'm sorry," she whispered, "I was only trying to help. You seem so hurt. I don't know what to do."

"I know, Aunt Vicki. I'm not sure what to do myself. I just need time to think. Time to breathe."

Vicki promised Shea right there she wouldn't butt in again.

"I know you're only trying to do your best for me. You're the first person since this happened that actually listened and I thank you for that."

Vicki knew she had to let Shea deal with this in her own way, although it hurt her to see her niece in so much pain. But she would not go back on her word.

The den door burst open and Shea stepped back in fright. Her cousin Ted entered. Shea stiffened as he grabbed her, twirling her around in a circle. Shea laughed in spite of herself. She had always adored Ted, he was like the big brother she never had.

"I heard you were here," he laughed, spinning her around. "Sorry I couldn't make it over last night." As he put her back down, he noticed the bruised lump on her forehead. "Shea, what happened?"

Shea tried to downplay her injury, not wanting to get into the details again. She mumbled it was nothing, but Ted wouldn't let up until she told him about it.

He was so mad when he found out, the veins stood out on both sides of his neck. She tried to calm him but he couldn't be consoled. Shea watched the blood redden his deeply tanned face. She sat him down and changed their conversation by asking about Peg, his wife. She was very soft spoken, always sweet to Shea. She was definitely a devoted wife to Ted.

Ted was good looking, with blond hair, blue eyes, and a deep tan from living in Florida. He was much taller, taking after Abbey and Caroline in the height department, but he took after his mother in personality. He was warm and charming and looked at life as an adventure. He didn't let things bother him much. He was, however a fierce protector. No one got away with hurting anyone in his family. Even as children when Shea came to visit, Ted took it upon himself to look after her. They adored each other and kept in touch often. Ted was a few years older than Shea so it was like she had her own older brother.

Shea was certainly glad he showed up when he did. It was the perfect time to change the subject and talk about something more cheery.

"Shea is staying for a while, Ted," interrupted Vicki.

"Great!" He put his arm around her. He'd calmed down some when he realized Shea didn't want to talk about the rape, but he vowed he'd get the details from his mother later.

They all made their way into the kitchen where Vicki had made fresh coffee. Ted and Shea talked and laughed. For the first time, Shea felt a little like her old self.

◆　　◆　　◆

Kevin looked across the table at Sarah, her hair glistening in the candlelight. He watched her sipping her wine and smiled to himself at her utter innocence. She was so naïve. That was what he was counting on, to get what he needed. He understood the rules well, not being new to smooth-talking young women. He was good at it and always put him where he needed to be. He understood the way the game was played and most women seemed to enjoy it. Make them feel wanted by lavishing gifts on them. Let them know he thought they are the most beautiful. To him, women were the most beautiful creatures in the world. Especially when they were being seduced.

His plan was working well, but he had to nurture the conversation. It was up to him to lead where he wanted to go. He had no need to worry because he'd done this many times before. He ran most of his life, sweet-talking his way out of one bend after another.

Sarah felt giddy. A warm sensation was working its way from her toes through her limbs and into the pit of her stomach. She let a small giggle escape and quickly covered her mouth to hide it. "I really didn't think you'd call me again," she said, suppressing a grin.

"Are you happy I did?" She nodded. "How's the wine?" He watched in amusement as it took its effect on her.

Sarah sat back lazily against the chair. "The wine is wonderful." She heard herself gush and tried to cover her drunkenness, quickly sitting back up.

"I see we're going to have to feed you to straighten you out," he smiled. They had already ordered their meal.

"Don't be silly," she cooed. "I'm fine." Sarah felt she was the luckiest girl alive. She looked around the restaurant in awe. She had nabbed a good one and felt proud. Kevin was very handsome and no one could dispute the fact he had money, for he had no problem spending it on her. She'd received another bouquet of flowers the day after the first set, and he brought her a gift back from his business trip. She couldn't help dreaming of future business trips, which she hoped she'd accompany him. He was more than interested in her, she could clearly see that.

She felt the same toward him, but the nagging question still churned deep inside her. She had to know for sure. She wasn't sure how she'd get the guts to ask him, but she knew if she kept drinking, the courage would come. She was just about to say something when he surprised her with a question.

"Where do you see this relationship going?" he asked sheepishly.

The question was so sudden, it caught Sarah off guard. She didn't expect a question like that from someone like him. She stumbled for an answer, wondering if she should tell him she was crazy about him. No boys her own age had ever made her feel this way. She wanted to cry out, 'I love you,' but composed herself to give an answer she thought would suit him. "I feel there's a lot of potential," she replied nervously.

"Well, that's wonderful!" he blurted out.

Surprised, Sarah turned to the stares that were coming from the other patrons. She blushed and giggled.

"I'm serious, Sarah. You make me feel great. I love just watching you. I just...."

"What?"

Kevin paused, purposefully watching for the look he wanted. Seeing it in her eyes, he continued. "I just don't want you to think I'm too old for you, that's all. If you think I am, just say so...."

"No, silly." She reached out to him. "That's just it. I like you. You're not like other men I've dated. I feel so special when I'm with you."

"Good." He was content, his ploy working.

The waitress brought their meals. She tied a bib around Sarah's neck and served her the lobster crackers.

Kevin smiled at her. "You sure you can handle those things?"

She laughed with confidence. "Yes, I've had lobster lots of times. I'm an old pro."

He let out a hardy laugh. They had settled in to eat when Sarah put her fork down and looked at him seriously. If she didn't ask now she knew she never would. "Can I ask you something?" she finally said in all seriousness.

Uneasy, Kevin looked at her, shifting in his chair. "Sure, it's only fair. I ask you something, you ask me...." He stopped when he saw the serious look on her face. He suspected he already knew what she was going to say.

"What happened the night we took Shea home?" she blurted out before she lost her nerve.

"What do you mean?" he asked innocently, trying not to let the fright show on his face.

"I fell asleep. What happened after that?"

Kevin took a sip of wine and placed the glass back on the table. Leaning forward on his elbows he was careful not to talk too loud. "Well, after you went to sleep, Shea and I talked. She said she wanted to go home instead of your house, because she had some things to do in the morning. So I dropped her off home."

Sarah thought about what he had said. Shea begged her mother to take her home too and she had been planning to go out the following morning. So far, his story seemed legitimate.

"Your cousin is quite a character," he continued. "We talked a little bit. She told me about her parents." Sarah had a look of confusion on her face that Kevin read well. Her mood lightened when he told her Shea had admitted not liking him when she'd gotten in the truck. "She was real concerned about you. I told her you were just out enjoying your graduation." He laughed, and Sarah smiled. He was doing such a good job, he was beginning to believe the story himself. He saw Sarah's face soften and he continued. "You know, she said she was actually jealous of you." Sarah looked at him, stunned. "Really!" he insisted convincingly. "She said she sometimes envied the fact you didn't have a boyfriend to answer to."

"Shea said that?" Sarah took a drink of wine. "That doesn't sound like her. She adores Billy."

Kevin thought he might have gone too far. "You know I don't think she meant what she said," he corrected. "Sometimes you wish you were in someone else's shoes. Don't you ever wish that?" He attempted to take the emphasis off his last statement.

Sarah thought about it for a moment. "Yeah, I guess you're right." She felt satisfied with his answer, turning her attention back to the claw she was cracking. She felt his hand touch her face, and she drew her eyes to him.

"Are you okay?" he asked, almost believing he was truly concerned.

Sarah nodded half-heartedly. "Shea said you attacked her," she burst out. "I just don't know why she'd say such a thing."

"Sarah, all I can tell you is what I know. She said she wanted to go home, so I took her. When we got there, there was a car in the driveway. I asked her if she wanted me to see who it was but she said she knew them. She got out of the truck and that was it." He held out his hands in a gesture of honesty. "Sarah, I wouldn't hurt Shea or Billy." Sarah looked at him with wide eyes and her mouth slightly open. "Can I tell you something?" he asked.

Sarah shrugged her shoulders. "Sure."

"You have to promise me you won't say a thing to anyone. Not even your mother."

She shook her head. "I promise."

"You've got to promise."

"I promise, Kevin," Sarah insisted, a little irritated.

Kevin reached into his front pocket and pulled out a card. He laid it on the table in front of Sarah. She took the card and read it. The name caught her attention right away. '*Jared Kevin Kendall.*'

"What does this mean?" She held the card out to him.

Kevin took the card back, laughing. "What it means is I'm Billy's half-brother."

Sarah had known about the two older Kendalls but no one really talked about them. They were so much older than the two younger Kendalls. She'd even heard the story about Jake and Naomi, but never paid attention to it. Kevin grabbed her attention again.

"Sarah?" She looked at him. "That's why I'm so concerned about both of them. I love my brother, I wouldn't do anything to hurt him. Now look, you got to promise me you won't say anything. I'm going to see the family soon but I want to surprise them." She nodded again. "I know something happened that night. I've been checking around town and I know Billy's real upset and looking for Shea. I also know she left. Sarah, I don't want to say anything bad about your cousin, but that car parked in her driveway was full of boys. She looked like she was having a good time with them. My brother deserves better than that."

Sarah was caught up in a whirlwind, not knowing what to do. This was all coming so fast, the truth about who Kevin was and these stories about her cousin who she thought she knew so well. But there had been a group of boys that night. The hospital said so. How could Kevin know this if he didn't see it for himself? Deep down she had never believed Kevin could be capable of rape. Shea had been lying about him. But what about Billy? She knew Shea loved him. She thought about their conversation in the bathroom that night at the Icehouse. Could it really be true that Shea wanted to break off the relationship with Billy? Suddenly she was jolted back again.

"Sarah?" whispered Kevin.

She shook her head is if to chase something out of it. "What?"

"I need your help with Billy."

"How?" She scrunched up her face.

"I know Billy's hurting right now, he sure could use a friend. Look, I've got to go out of town again for a few days. Do me a favor and befriend Billy. Ask him to the movies or dinner. You know, make him feel better."

Sarah shook her head. "I don't know Kevin. I mean Jared."

"Call me Kevin," he corrected.

"Billy and I never really got along that well."

"Come on, Billy gets along with everyone. Just find something to keep his mind occupied."

Sarah thought for a moment. "My mom did want me to do something with that old patch of dirt in the back yard. Maybe I'll get Billy to help me with that."

"That sounds great. But don't forget about me," he scolded.

Sarah giggled. Whatever reservations she had before, Kevin certainly had a way of making her forget.

60

"You really are special, Sarah." He caressed her cheek with his thumb. Her whole body broke out in a tingle. She leaned into his touch and kissed the palm of his hand.

CHAPTER SIX

Sarah headed toward Billy, who was stacking crates in the corner of the warehouse. He looked tired and depressed, like someone who'd just lost his best friend. He looked so sad, Sarah felt for him. He was lost without Shea. Thinking back to the conversation with Kevin the night before, she still wondered if it could be true. How did Kevin know so much about the story if it wasn't?

She knew her job was to make Billy feel better, but she was nervous. Knowing how close he was to Shea, it was going to be difficult to make him forget easily. She doubted that she alone could make any difference.

Kevin had enlisted her help to keep Shea away from Billy at all costs. She'd gone the past few mornings and checked the mailbox for any letters from Shea, something Kevin had asked her to do. All this checking around and lying was proving to be tougher than she thought, but she felt it was worth it. She thought it was wonderful Kevin cared so much about his brother he would go to any length to keep any bad news from Shea away from him. Sarah wondered what on earth she was going to say to Billy. The way he looked she knew nothing was going to change his mood. She took a deep breath and walked across to where he was standing. "Billy!" she called across the hall.

Billy stopped what he was doing and looked up. She thought she saw a glimmer of hope rise in his eyes, which made it even harder for her to talk to him. But she'd already gotten his attention and now she was stuck. She smiled nervously and walked over to greet him.

"Sarah, hi. How are things going?"

She was saddened by his grim demeanor. She and Billy only shared one thing in common and that was Shea. She could tell by his

62

tone where the conversation was heading. She braced herself for the inevitable question.

"Has anyone heard from Shea?" he asked, right on cue.

Sarah shook her head. "No," she lied. "I would have thought you'd have gotten a letter by now." She didn't know what else to say at that point. She wanted to blurt out what Kevin had told her, but she promised not to mention he was in town. She remembered what he said about letting him down gently.

Sarah quickly changed the subject. "Billy, I need help with something. My Mom has asked me to fill in that dirt spot in the back yard." She rambled on about the plot of dirt and what she had in mind. She was hoping Billy couldn't see how nervous she was.

"What kind of flowers did you have in mind?" he asked hesitantly. He was beginning to realize Sarah and her family wouldn't be much help in his quest to find Shea. He knew they were hiding something, every time he'd called Caroline, she was short and to the point, then made excuses to get off the phone quickly. He decided days ago, if he wanted to find out anything, he'd have to do it himself. He just couldn't understand why everyone was being so secretive. He figured Shea must have gone to her aunt's in Florida, but he hadn't kept her address. When he called information, there were over one hundred Smiths in the phone book in Miami. No one in Shea's family would give him the information he needed. He was determined to keep looking. Somehow he'd find her, he promised himself.

Billy shook his head when he realized Sarah was talking to him. "What?"

"I said I thought tulips would be nice." Her voice had grown agitated, more from lying to him than his obvious preoccupation with Shea.

He shrugged his shoulders and led her through the rows of flowering plants. He helped her select a few that would be easy to care for. A few more times he attempted to bring up the subject of Shea. Each time it was thwarted.

He thought about the phone call they had the night she disappeared. Maybe what he had been feeling the past few weeks wasn't his imagination. But then why had they planned to go away for their special weekend? Why would she even suggest it. That, too, she had said she wanted. Maybe it was just too soon and she didn't want to deal with it. But it wasn't like Shea at all. They were so open about everything. No, something wasn't making sense, here. There were a lot of questions roaming around in his head and he intended to find answers for them. He rang up Sarah's order, then helped her to the car with the load of plants.

Sarah got in and started the car up. She wanted to leave quickly but the look on Billy's face made her stop. "Billy, I'm sure Shea will be getting in touch with you soon," she tried to reassure him. "Please try not to worry about her too much."

He leaned against the car. "I just want to know if she's okay. See, we kind of had a fight on the phone that night."

Sarah fell back with her head against the headrest. "She told me about the phone call. Shea is fine, but she needed time away. She had some problems to work out." Sarah reached out and touched his hand. "Billy, try not to worry. I know she'll be getting in touch with you very soon." She rolled up the window and started to leave.

"But, Sarah...." Billy tried to get her tell him more but she drove away.

When she looked back she could see Billy standing in the middle of the parking lot, looking like a lost puppy that needed a hug. Sarah drove faster to get away from him. She really did sympathize with him, but if what Kevin said was true, then she knew she was doing him a favor.

Shea had been acting peculiarly lately, Sarah thought. She'd spent most of Sarah's graduation party up in her room. Then there was the fight with her mother. She wondered what brought that on and why would Kevin lie to her anyway. He'd never even seen Shea before the night they brought her home. She refused to believe anything bad about Kevin. He was so wonderful to her, different from any other relationship she'd been in.

She thought longingly about Kevin and the times she'd spent with him since they met. Shea was just jealous, that was it. Shea wanted what Sarah had so she made up a terrible story about Kevin. Sarah finally felt vindicated. That would explain why Shea said the things she did. All the confusion she'd felt the past few days was slipping away. She felt better than she had since it all first happened.

◆　　◆　　◆

Kevin nervously tapped the table with the end of his fork. The waitress brought him his coffee and took his order. He stirred in the cream and waited impatiently. He saw Greg make his way across the restaurant and slide in the booth across from him. He handed him the envelope without saying a word, and Kevin took a yellow envelope out from his coat and gave it to Greg. Opening his envelope, Kevin thumbed through the information.

"Sorry it's so late," said Greg. "My informant at the hospital was off for a few days and just got back yesterday." Kevin looked at him in surprise. "Don't worry. She got the information before she left. She's been holding it at her place."

"Is it all here?" Kevin looked up at Greg.

He nodded. "Look," he fidgeted. "I can get in a lot of trouble for this. I only did it because it's your brother."

Kevin reached across the table and shook his hand. "I'm doing it for him too. I only want to protect my brother from this horrible story. He loved that girl so much. She didn't deserve him. If the only thing I can do is keep this story from the newspapers it's all worth it. Now, you're sure no one knows about this?"

Greg nodded again. "But what about Sarah?" he asked.

Kevin snickered. "We don't have to worry about her. She's on our side." Greg gave a nod and poured some cream into the coffee the waitress had set in front of him. "So, Kevin, how long you been back in town?"

"Oh, couple of days or so. Came back to help my dad. He's not doing so well, you know?" Greg nodded in acknowledgment. "I didn't think I'd be helping my little brother out of a jam, too. You know, I gave that girl a ride home that night. She talked about Billy all the way there and then got in a car with a bunch of boys right in front of me!"

Greg shook his head. "You know, she always played so inno-cent like she and Billy were an item." He leaned in close to Kevin and whispered in a low voice. "I always suspected something with her, you know. Like, I asked her out a few times, and she said no, she was going steady. But I heard things from other boys at school. You know, like things that would happen at the basketball games'n stuff."

Kevin listened intently for a moment. "And that's why I have to protect my little brother. If you let them, girls will try and get away with anything. I tell ya, you can't trust them."

Greg gave a wide grin. "I always say use them, then lose them. Otherwise they got ya for life."

Kevin winked in agreement. "You got that right."

Greg excused himself, then left. Kevin sat back with a smile of triumph on his face and swallowed what remained of his coffee.

CHAPTER SEVEN

Shea walked into the den and curled up on the couch, shivering. Vickie saw how cold she was and covered her with a blanket. Her niece had been like this close to a week, now.

"This isn't right, your not feeling well, like this," she commented.

"I feel sick to my stomach. I just don't know what's wrong with me." Shea curled up deeper under the blankets. "I'm so tired all the time!"

Vickie suspected she knew what might be wrong. Shea gagged at the slightest smell of anything. A few more symptoms would prove it. She sat beside her and placed a hand on her forehead.

"Have you noticed anything different about your body, Shea?"

Frowning, Shea looked down at herself. "If it's at all possible, I'd swear my breasts have gotten bigger. Like overnight. I feel like I'm going to get my period."

"When is it due?"

Shea thought for a moment. "This week sometime. I'm not sure, it's so irregular." Her face suddenly registered doubt. Vickie realized Shea had had her own suspicions about her condition. She reached out and enveloped her niece in her arms.

"It wasn't supposed to happen like this," sputtered Shea. "I was going to marry Billy. We were going to have a baby together, we had it all planned." She broke free from her aunt, slamming a fist against the couch. "I can't be pregnant, Aunt Vickie! What am I going to do?"

Vickie felt a cold anger toward Shea's rapist. It was bad enough that the rape had taken place at all, but now for this to happen. "Shea," she said quietly, "I want you to understand that none of this was your fault." She knew from her days of working in the emergency room that rape victims invariably blamed themselves for the crime. "That man violated you in the worst way possible. He had no right to do what he did. He's the bad guy, not you. You did nothing to deserve being raped."

"I got in the car with him," answered Shea through gritted teeth. "How could I have been so stupid?"

"Don't blame yourself for that, you said yourself you did it to help Sarah."

"Yeah, and now Sarah's walking around probably with the rest of the town calling me a liar! Why was it not her? Why did it have to happen to me?"

"Shea, you've got to believe me, none of this was your fault. I don't know why it happened to you and not Sarah. I suppose if I did we'd know why there are monsters out there that do these hideous things, but you had nothing to deserve what happened to you." Vickie took Shea's hands in hers, looking her straight in the eye. "Listen, my dear... I've left you alone to deal with this in your own way, but I think you should talk to a friend of mine. He's a therapist. I don't want to push you, but I believe he could help you sort this all out."

Shea got up and paced the floor. "Maybe he could help me figure it out."

"I know he can at least help," said Vickie, standing up. "Maybe if you just talked with him once... if you don't want to go back I won't say another word about it." She paused for a beat. "Shea, I hate to bring this up too, but...." She nodded toward her niece's stomach.

"Okay," said Shea wearily, "I'll make an appointment for both tomorrow."

Vickie hugged her. "I'll go with you, if you like. We'll get through this together."

The tests the next day confirmed what they already knew. Getting pregnant had never even crossed Shea's mind. The nurses at the doctor's office were very understanding, sympathizing with her plight. One even gave her information on abortion, which startled Shea. Never in her wildest dreams had she thought about having an abortion, but now as she sat in the therapist's office, she took the pamphlet out to read.

One saving grace about the whole thing was that after she found out she was pregnant, she didn't connect the horrible man who forced himself on her with the new life growing inside her. She felt they had nothing to do with each other.

When the therapist came out of his office, Shea studied him carefully. His slightly graying hair was combed perfectly off to one side. He had wonderfully soft features and piercing blue eyes which put Shea immediately at ease. She wondered if there might be more than friendship between he and Aunt Vickie.

As he introduced himself, she couldn't help but notice the soft timbre of his voice. She was glad she had made the appointment. He carried an air about him that said he could take care of her.

◆   ◆   ◆

It had been six weeks since Shea found out she was pregnant. She'd written Billy three letters but hadn't received a single response. So many times she was tempted to pick up the phone and call him. But she still wasn't ready to answer the questions she knew he'd ask. There were probably rumors racing around town about her. Maybe Billy had decided he was better off without her. She really couldn't blame him, she wasn't sure she could have handled the situation if she were in his shoes. These were all problems she was working out with her counselor, Dr. Riggs. They seemed to be making some headway, but Shea knew this was an experience she would never be able to forget.

Vicki had been so gracious in not pushing her. She had given Shea space to figure out the one question that hummed in her head day and night. Why her and not Sarah? Why had she gotten in the truck in the first place? If only she hadn't, she'd be at college, settling in and looking for a job. The doctor told her not to focus on the why. It was a question she probably could never answer, anyway.

Shea decided she needed to get out and do something, so she signed up for classes at the local college. She could not let the rape interfere with her goals to finish school.

The therapist was surprised to hear she was starting school, and encouraged her to work on things that might help her put her life back together.

Shea sat in the college cafeteria, filling out her forms. For the first time in a while, she felt positive about her life.

Feeling the table shift, she looked up to see a sandy haired man staring down at her. At first he looked nervous, but when he introduced himself, he smiled, putting Shea at ease. He had a warm, friendly glow with mischievous blue eyes above prominent cheekbones.

"Filling out the application?" he asked, his white teeth gleaming.

Shea nodded, rolling her eyes to indicate she found the forms tedious.

"My name's Steven," he held out his hand. "Here, let me help you with those." He sat in the chair next to Shea and pointed out some short cuts to filling out the form. "This is my second year. I've been through all this before."

They talked for a while. Shea began to relax, knowing she had someone to show her the ropes. She felt good that she was finally putting her life back in some sense of order. She'd read about rape victims who got so depressed, they weren't even able to get out of bed. But not her.

Steve showed her where the bookstore was, then went with her to register. He even signed up for one of the classes she was in, so they could study together.

Promising to meet him in the parking lot the next day, she went to her car. The top was down on her convertible as she drove out. The sun beat down on her, and the warm ocean breeze made her feel serene and secure. She was going to like it, here. She had her Aunt Vicki and cousin Ted, who were very supportive. Now she'd met a new friend to take classes with. Despite the continuous gnawing feeling she had in her stomach, things were getting better.

When Shea got home that afternoon, she searched through the mail again. She did this every day, hoping for word from Billy. Again, there was no letter for her, but today somehow it seemed less important. She was moving on. School started in a few days, and she had found Steve to help her through the first few days of class. However, Billy would never be far from her thoughts, she missed him terribly. Why hadn't he written? Maybe he was just as at a loss as she.

She hadn't planned on staying permanently in Florida, but she realized she couldn't go back now. Not after she decided to keep the baby. New Salem would never understand and it would only lead to more speculation about what really happened that night. Shea still couldn't accept the fact that her attacker was running around free as a bird. She could never face seeing him. Anyway, she needed her aunt, Vicki being the only one Shea felt comfortable with.

Going back to New Salem was out of the question. Even Billy may not understand her decision to keep a child who was conceived from rape. Knowing how small towns thought, she would be mercilessly gossiped about. Maybe that was why she didn't call Billy, he didn't deserve the embarrassment she would cause him. Maybe he was better off without her.

◆　　　◆　　　◆

As Naomi opened the door, her heart froze. She said nothing, peering at the tall figure darkening the steps.

"Hi, Naomi. Is my dad here?" Kevin pushed past her.

She closed the door, heading down the hall. "Wait here," she ordered icily as she passed Kevin. She had tried over the years to make friends with him, but he had never liked her and she didn't trust him. She knew about his past and all the problems he had caused his father, Jake.

Kevin waited in the kitchen. Cautiously he thumbed through the mail lying on the table. Nothing from Shea. When he heard Naomi returning, he quickly put the envelopes back in a pile.

"He's in the den," she said, going to the stove without looking at him.

Kevin entered the den where his father sat in a recliner. He looked much older and very pale, Kevin was surprised at the bad turn Jake had taken. The den looked almost the same as it had when Kevin had lived there. There were new pictures, of course, banishing the ones of his first family. The room was dark except for a small table lamp and the soft flickering of the television. His dad was covered up like a small, sick child.

With a shaking hand, Jake motioned him to sit. Kevin took the

71

chair on the opposite side of the room, facing him. His dad picked up the remote, lowering the volume on the television.

"Hi, Dad," said Kevin in a happy tone.

As Jake tried to sit up, Kevin rushed to help him. "It's been a long time, Jared," said Jake in a weak voice.

Kevin sat back down. He hadn't been called by that name in a long time. Leaning forward in his seat, he twiddled his thumbs. It was an awkward moment. He wanted to get back in the company, but he needed his father's trust. This meeting had to be handled with kid gloves.

"I'm sorry I've stayed away so long, Dad. With all the problems I've caused in the past, I figured it was better." He kept his head bowed, waiting for his dad's response.

"You're still my son," said Jake shakily. "I may not always agree with the things you do, but you're always welcome to come back home. I hope you have some good news for me."

Kevin smiled. "I'm glad to hear you say that," he answered. "I've really tried to clean up my act these past few years. I know I caused you a lot of heartache. I want to make it up to you, show you I'm different."

Jake held his hand up. "You've done good, son. Why have you come back?"

Kevin stood. His father was never one for small talk. That was Jake, to the point... he pulled no punches. Kevin paced the floor, searching for the right words. Knowing he couldn't sweet-talk his dad, he thought it best to come right to the point. "Dad, I need a job. I know you're not going to the shop every day... and well, I thought Billy might need help."

Jake was silent for a long moment. He pulled himself up, speaking softly from sheer exhaustion. His heart condition left him gasping for air most of the time, now. "I promised all my kids they would have a place in my company. It belongs to you all, anyway," he stumbled. "I've put away a tidy sum for Naomi and me, but I never thought you were that much interested in the shop." His voice grew harsh. "You and your sister, Brenda, seemed to have gone off on your own." After a pause, he went on. "I can't deny you a place in the business, but you don't know that much about it, Jared. I'll tell you what. You can work at the shop under one condition...."

Kevin perked up. He thought it was going to be much more difficult than this. "What's that?" he asked, folding his hands in front of him.

"As you probably know, Billy is running the shop. He's had the experience and he knows what he's doing. You can work there if he remains in charge." Kevin began to interrupt, but his dad cut him off. "That's it, Jared. You don't have enough experience, yet. Let Billy teach you."

Kevin reluctantly agreed. He had to admit his father was right, Billy did know what the business was all about. He decided to let his half-brother show him the ropes, then edge him out when the time came. Maybe this would work out after all, he smiled to himself. That way he could keep an eye on the situation with Shea, too. Kevin was pleased with himself. His visit went better than he hoped it would. It was a surprise that his dad seemed pleased him to have him back in town, and open to him working in the shop. That was more than Kevin could have hoped for.

Kevin called Sarah to tell her the news. It was time to move onto the next stage of his plan. He wondered how she was doing with Billy. Kevin wasn't sure how he felt about Sarah. She had a definite hold on him and it bothered him that he felt out of control with her so much of the time. It was like she was willing to be manipulated, but only on her terms. It made him uncomfortable to find himself wanting to be with her more and more.

Even so, Kevin felt pleased with his progress so far. He couldn't have gotten any luckier picking up his brother's girlfriend that night. He thought Shea had been coming on to him when she got in the truck, the way she looked at him. He hadn't meant for it to get out of hand, but he could swear she asked for it. Then when she rejected him, he lost it. He couldn't dwell on it, though. He had a plan and it was time to put his hard work into play. The warehouse he'd negotiated for was in place and the equipment companies were already making deliveries. This was going to be so

73

easy. He congratulated himself. He would go to work with Billy every day, sell merchandise off the floor, but have it delivered from his warehouse. The customers would never know the merchandise wasn't coming off the Garden Centers floor, and Kevin would make the profit. He had already arranged to have any sales delivered directly to the customers' homes. Things were going like a dream. Heck, it sure beat robbing, he laughed to himself.

CHAPTER EIGHT

6 months later

Billy sat alone in the darkness of the den, wondering where everything had gone so wrong. He blamed himself. If he'd just been more attentive toward Shea. But he had thought she knew what he was up against in taking over the business.

There were so many unanswered questions. Now he was not sure he wanted to know the answers. Why hadn't Shea written? What had he done? Or was it what people said all along would happen... she grew up and found someone else?

She certainly had had enough time since they graduated. Billy had worked almost all the time. Had she been lying to him? If she was unhappy, why hadn't she said something? They always talked about everything. He remembered their conversation on the phone the night she disappeared. He thought then there was something wrong, now he berated himself for not pursuing the talk longer. Now he'd never find out how Shea was feeling.

What he couldn't understand is why everyone was so secretive about her leaving. And Sarah never came around anymore. When he did see her, she changed the subject the minute he alluded to Shea. There were some stories about Shea in town, but he was so busy he never had time to check any of them out. Everything was coming down on him so fast and so hard.

Shea should have said something. Both of them had a responsibility to speak up and say what was bothering them. It had always been that way between them. Billy heard someone coming. Quickly, he wiped away an unshed tear.

Naomi switched on the light. "I'm sorry, Billy. I didn't realize there was anyone in here. I ah...was just wanting to put this book back." She waited for a moment, looking at Billy with concern.

Even she was confused about what had happened. She and

Shea had been so close, she couldn't imagine why she just left like that. It hurt Naomi to see her son so upset.

"It's okay, Mom. You can come in, I need to talk to you, anyway."

She came into the room. "Are you okay?" she asked, noticing the dried tear stains on his face.

Billy bowed his head. "I suppose I will be."

Naomi sat down on the hassock next to her son. "It's Shea, isn't it?"

He nodded. "You all warned me, I didn't listen." Leaning back, he sighed. "Why couldn't I have listened?"

Naomi put her hand on Billy's arm. "I wish I had the answers, sweetie. I'm your mother, I thought I'd always be able to take your hurt away. I could when you were little. I'm supposed to have all the answers, but I don't. It rips my heart out to see you so hurt. I love Shea too, I feel bad she left." She paused. "Have you tried to find her?"

"I know where she is, In Florida. Where else would she go? I just don't know why."

"I suppose it doesn't help, right now, but in time the hurt will disappear."

"It'll never disappear. She'll always be in my heart, Mom. She was the only girl I've ever loved."

"You know, Shea was always like the daughter I never had. I loved her, too."

Billy sighed, "Another thing I don't understand is why everyone is being so secretive about her. Every time I ask Sarah anything, she just shrugs it off, telling me to forget about her. What happened, Mom?"

Naomi crawled up on the chair next to Billy. "Push over, son. I'm gonna do something I haven't done since you were a baby." Billy scooted to one side of the chair to let his mom next to him. She wrapped her arms around him, pulling him close to her. Gently, she laid his head down on her shoulder. "There, that's better. Now, I want you to tell me all about it. Your mama's listening."

Billy burst out laughing. "You know, this feels kinda good."

Naomi laughed too, and they talked long into the night.

◆　　　◆　　　◆

"So, did you get them?" Kevin demanded, pacing in front of her.

Sarah took the letters from her purse and threw them at Kevin. "I'm sick of playing your little spy, Kevin. If you want any more of these letters, you'll have to get them yourself!" She turned briskly to walk out but Kevin caught her arm.

"What's your problem, little miss? Not enough lovin' for you? Is that what you need, a good screwing?"

Sarah pulled her arm away. "No, I'm just sick of doing your dirty work. I almost got caught the other day, you know. Naomi came out and asked me what I was doing in her mailbox."

Kevin intently stared at her. "Well, what happened?"

"I told her I was looking for an ad or something."

"That was clever." He was surprised at her quick thinking.

" Yeah, well that's it. I'm not doing it anymore. Naomi still likes me, I don't want to ruin our relationship."

"Naomi likes everyone. Believe me, you won't get her mad by going through her mailbox."

"Well, nevertheless, count me out. If you want Billy's, mail you can get it yourself. I don't know why we have to do this anyway... so what if he finds out where she is?"

Kevin rolled his eyes. "Because, my dear, I've told you before. We don't want Billy having to face the truth about Shea."

"Why should we care if he finds out? Let the two of them work it out, it's not our problem anyway. Unless of course you're guilty of what Shea's accusing you of. Is that it? You're afraid Billy will find out the truth!"

Kevin spun around in a fury. "How dare you say such a thing! And you remember, princess, you're just as guilty as I am. If I go down, you go too. I'll bet you've never seen the inside of a jail before, have you?"

Sarah stared him down. "I'm guilty of nothing."

Kevin held the letters out in front of her, waving them ferociously. "Oh no, and what about these? Stealing mail is a federal offense, in case you haven't heard. That ought to put you away for...." He thought for a moment. "For a little while, anyway. Long enough to know you don't ever want to go back. Whether you want to be or not, miss princess, you're in this up to your elbows."

Sarah sank down into the chair, her head tucked in her fur coat. She wondered how she'd ever gotten herself into such a mess. All she wanted was someone to love her. When she met Kevin she thought she'd found her true love. Now his past was coming back to haunt them both. She was way into this and she didn't want to be. She wanted out, but how?

Kevin saw her expression and pulled her to him. "Hey," he whispered, wiping a tear from her face. "It's going to be okay. You have to believe what we're doing is right. All we're doing is giving Billy a chance to move on with his life. Sarah, you have to believe me. I really did see Shea leave with those boys that night. Now, if it were just her I'd say go for it... tell the whole town. But we're talking about my brother. He would be devastated. I will not let that tramp embarrass my family like that." He tilted her chin so she looked at him. "You remember who is at fault here, not me or you. It's certainly not Billy. It's Shea. Shea and only Shea." He smiled. "Now, I have a great idea that'll stop Shea from writing, and you won't have to look through the mail anymore."

Sarah gave him a questioning look. "What is it?" She'd be willing to do anything to be rid of whole situation.

Kevin led her to the couch, sitting her down on his lap. "Now, all you have to do is write a letter to Aunt Vicki, telling her Billy's getting married."

"How is that going to work?" she asked, shocked.

"Simple. You write that you know Shea will find out sooner or later, and that you figured it would be better if you told Shea yourself, first. You know, break it to her gently."

Sarah was silent for a moment. "I don't know. You don't know my Aunt Vicki like I do. She may decide not to tell Shea just so she can protect her."

"I don't think so. Especially if she knows Shea is still writing to Billy. Anyway, it's worth a try, then both of us can move on with our lives and forget about those two. They've come between us long enough."

Kevin was happy to see a smile slip across Sarah's face. He knew his little plan had set with her, he was back in the running again. She could be tough sometimes, but he never doubted her love for him. Reaching up, he kissed Sarah on the mouth. It started as a peck and grew into a long, passionate embrace. He swept her off the sofa and carried her into the bedroom. He had to admit this woman pretty much had him captured, too. He was definitely smitten with her youth and childlike innocence. The very scent of her close to him like this, made his heart beat faster. He ripped her coat off, laying her on the bed. Pushing the skirt of her dress up around her waist, he methodically peeled off her panties and plunged himself deep inside her.

She let out a gasping moan and thrust her hips to meet him. How she loved to feel him deep within her as they moved together as one. Fast and furious, she liked it that way. Like their life together. She wanted no other man. She knew that. Even with his sorted past, it just made him more alluring. She knew in her heart, she would do whatever he wanted, for she couldn't bear to lose him. Never again would she find another who filled every inch of her soul.

They came down slowly, resting beside each other. He kissed her tenderly, pulling her close to him. He loved being next to her, touching her and bringing her pleasure, the look in her eyes after they made love. She was like a drug to him, an all-consuming, addictive drug.

Sarah cuddled closer to Kevin and touched his penis. She hadn't been using birth control for some time now and wondered why she hadn't gotten pregnant. If she did, Kevin would have to marry her. Since the families were so close, it would be inevitable.

They made love every time they were together. Kevin had taken her to the doctor and even bought her the pills, but she'd stopped taking them months ago. She didn't care how angry he would be when he found out she had conceived. She was sure he would eventually calm down and accept his duties as a father. Then they would be married. She'd have her prince forever, not to mention the Kendall fortune to boot.

She worked to arouse him again, then climbed on top to take him. She'd done that often because Kevin liked it. Before long they were once more rocking, racing to their inevitable climax.

CHAPTER NINE

Shea stood at the mirror, staring at the huge mound that stuck out around her stomach. Again she winced as another contraction took hold. She'd been having them a lot the past week or so. The doctor told her not to worry, it was common the closer it got to the delivery date.

She'd finished one semester of school successfully. She was trying to decide if she should start again, but she only had a week left to register. She didn't want to miss any school if she could help it.

Steve had long since moved on. He had said it didn't bother him when he found out about the baby, but when she started showing he began making excuses why he couldn't study with her. Shea understood and relieved him of the drudgery of facing her straight out. She couldn't really blame him. It didn't bother her as much as she thought it would, this life inside her had become all that was important. She lived every day for the unborn child she carried. Now she had a purpose to finish school, everything she did was for the sake of her baby.

She didn't think about the rape much anymore. She'd stopped seeing the therapist on a professional basis, but as he still came around to see Aunt Vicki he was still a part of her life. He had been impressed at how quickly her attitude changed when she realized she was going to have a baby.

Making her way to the kitchen, she stopped mid-point to ward off another contraction. When she got to the kitchen, she joined Vicki, sitting at the table reading a letter.

"Hi, Aunt Vic, what are you reading?" She thumbed through the other envelopes.

Vicki sighed. "You'd better sit down, honey."

"What is it?" Shea pulled out the seat next to her aunt. "Someone die or something?"

Vicki shook her head. "No." She handed the letter to Shea. "This came from Sarah, today. She says Billy is getting married."

Stunned, Shea scanned through it reading how Sarah thought she should hear it from her before she found out from someone else. *'You don't know her, she's from Albany.'* Shea put the letter down on the table. She stared blindly for a moment before running from the room.

Hearing the bathroom door slam, Vicki followed. Shea was retching violently. Vicki pounded on the door. "Shea, open up."

Shea threw the door open, twisting back to crouch over the toilet bowl. "I think I'm in labor!" she sobbed.

"You can't be," Vicki said more for her own piece of mind than Shea's. "It's too soon, you still have a month left."

Shea wiped her mouth with the back of her hand. "No, it's true. I've been having bad contractions."

"What?" Her aunt helped her straighten. "We have to get you to the hospital. Why didn't you tell me this?"

Bent over, Shea staggered with Vicki's help to the garage. "The doctor said it was normal to have contractions," she managed.

"Okay." Vicki settled her in the car. "We'll get you to the hospital. Don't worry, everything's going to be fine." She rushed around to the driver's side and peeled out of the driveway. The way Shea sounded, she thought she was going to have the baby right there in the car. Vicki sped quickly, running through stop lights whenever feasible. When they reached the hospital, she pulled up in front of the emergency room doors.

"Come on honey, you've got to help me," pleaded Vicki, trying to help her niece from the car.

Shea tried to move but another contraction forced her back into the seat. She tried again, making it inside the hospital doors. Vicki grabbed an abandoned wheelchair in the hall and put Shea in it. Pushing her to where the reception desk was, she called, "Somebody help me!"

A nurse quickly dropped what she was doing and called for a doctor. Soon Shea was being wheeled off on a gurney.

"She's only at thirty-six weeks, doctor," said Vicki as they raced to the delivery room. A look of concern flashed over the doctor's face. Catching his expression, Shea panicked. "You've got to help my baby," she begged. Another contraction sent her into a frenzy. A mass of confusion erupted in the room. "Doctor, the baby's crowning! It's breach!" announced the nurse, her voice shrill with fear.

◆   ◆   ◆

Shea opened her eyes and looked around the room. Seeing her awake, Vicki jumped up to the bed.

"My baby...."

"Shhh," soothed Vicki, pulling the covers up around Shea's shoulders. "Your baby's fine. They have him in an incubator, but the doctor says he's going to be fine. He can probably come out of the incubator tonight. It was a difficult birth; the doctor had to sedate you." She smiled, tousling Shea's hair. "So, Mommy, how are we feeling?"

Shea tried to sit up. "Ow," she winced. "A little sore and a lot tired."

"Well, why don't you rest? I think they're going to be bringing him by soon."

Shea beamed at her aunt. "I can't wait to see him."

"I asked them if he was okay, could you keep him in your room," Vicki told her. "I also hired you your own private duty nurse."

"Aunt Vicki!" objected Shea. "You shouldn't have."

"Nonsense. It's my present to you. Besides, he's so beautiful. I want you to be able to be with him whenever you want."

Shea took her aunt's hand. "Thank you, Aunt Vicki. I could have never done any of this without you. I dread to think where I might be if it weren't for you."

Vicki kissed her niece's forehead. "Shea, you've always been like a daughter to me." The door opened and one of the hospital nurses came in. Vicki turned around. "Where's Shea's nurse?"

"Don't worry," smiled the nurse. "She'll be here shortly. I handpicked her myself. She used to be one of the top nurses on the floor. Maybe you remember her, Louise Peabody."

A look of surprise appeared on Vicki's face and she squealed with delight. "Oh, you got Lou to come back? How on earth?" She had worked with Louise for years when they both ran the baby ward. They were on separate shifts, but passed notes to one another through the other nurses. The two of them had kept that ward running like clockwork, both very strict with the staff, but they were respected and liked.

Just then Louise entered the room. "Okay," she barked, "now, I want some quiet in here. We have a sleeping baby on the way, you know."

Vicki gave her a huge hug. The two stood in the middle of the room for a few minutes carrying on about the 'good old days.'

"Oh dear, it's been so long. How have you been?"

Shea watched in delight as the two laughed and squealed with old stories. But she could hardly contain herself. She was dying to see her baby boy!

"I'm sorry," said Vicki finally. "Where are my manners? Lou, this is my niece, Shea."

Louise stepped forward and took Shea's hand tightly. Shea wondered secretly if this was going to be a good idea. Louise looked like she'd whipped a few good families into shape. She was heavy set and wore her hair in a bun like some of the teachers Shea had seen in grade school. When she grasped Shea's hand, it was with quite a grip. But there was a lovely softness in her amber brown eyes.

"Did your aunt tell you I'm going home with you?" she demanded with a grin.

"No, she didn't."

"Well, I am." She laughed heartily.

A baby's cry distracted all of them as Shea's son was finally wheeled into the room. Louise went to his bassinet. "I guess this is where I come in." She picked the squirming bundle up and carried him to Shea. "Does this little fella have a name?"

At last! Shea took him and cradled him close. She looked him over, taking in his perfect little features. She still couldn't believe the tiny creature belonged to her.

"His name is Ben," she announced. "Benjamin Oliver Parks."
Vicki pulled the blanket back from his face. "Why, he looks just like a Ben too."

Louise was all business. "Well, what I think is this little guy wants to eat. So, if you'll do the honors, Miss Shea."

Shea pulled the gown away from her breast and placed Ben up close. The baby immediately started suckling. "Look, he knows what to do," she said in awe.

The nurse snickered. "Oh, they're pretty intuitive."

Vicki and Louise left the room for a break while Shea fed her son. She took his little hand and kissed his forehead. He was so delicate, such a miracle. The memory of that terrible night when he was first conceived was erased from her memory, replaced by the thoughts of the new little baby she cradled in her arms.

She never once regretted her decision to keep her child. No one would have blamed her if she'd chosen to have an abortion, but she didn't think about that.

◆　　　◆　　　◆

Billy checked the mailbox again. He'd done that every day since Shea had disappeared. Still, no letter from her. He pulled up into the drive and sat for a minute before going in. It had been a while since he'd been able to get any time off, but with Kevin now working for the shop, Billy was able to get away.

He turned when he heard a car pulling in the drive behind him. It was Sarah. What was she doing here? He got out of his truck, hoping she had some news about Shea. Even though it had been well over eight months, he still he hoped she would someday come back.

"Hi, Sarah. What's up?"

She got out of her car and strolled up to him. "Is your brother here?" She carefully scrutinized Billy's face.

Billy looked at her, confused. "Michael?"

"No, silly. Kevin."

"What do you want with Kevin?" Billy wondered what he was up to, now.

"We're dating. I wondered where he was." It felt good to say those words. She'd been waiting so long to tell everyone, but Kevin had made her promise not to until he met with the family. He'd been back in town for over three months before contacting them.

Billy was taken aback. His brother had been back for five months now, he wasn't aware Kevin even knew Sarah. He hadn't been able to see or talk to his family much, with the business going gang-busters like it was. Still, it surprised him that Kevin would even consider going out with Sarah, she was so much younger than he.

"You're dating Kevin?"

"Yes, for some time now." Sarah knew Kevin was back at the shop, not here. She really just wanted to see how Billy was doing. She felt sorry for him. He still seemed so depressed.

"Well, Kevin's at the shop. Sarah, do you think it's a good idea to go out with him? After all, he's twice your age."

"He's good for me," she smiled. "We have a great time together."

"What about college?"

"I can still go to college if I want. I'm only going out with your brother, not married or pregnant." She glanced back at the mailbox. "Have you heard from Shea?" She wanted to know if any of the letters had gotten past her.

"No, have you?"

"No," she shrugged nonchalantly.

"You know, I would have thought I'd at least have heard something from her," Billy hoped for a response. "I know where she is," he said curtly.

Sarah's eyes grew big. "You do?"

"She's at your aunt's in Florida."

"How come you haven't tried to call her?" she asked nervously.

"How do you know I haven't?"

"Well, have you?"

"No, but I don't think you're telling me everything you know either."

Sarah leaned against her car and pulled her coat around her. "Look, Billy. I don't know much at all. I do know she kept in touch with a guy down there."

Billy frowned. "What are you trying to say, Sarah?"

She shrugged. "I'm not trying to say anything. All I know is I see you day after day chasing a hope that maybe isn't there. When are you going to get on with your life? It's been over eight months. I'm sure if Shea had wanted to talk to you she would have gotten hold of you by now."

Billy stomped off into the house, leaving Sarah standing in the cold wind by herself. A part of him knew she was right, but he just couldn't face the idea of going on without Shea. He felt like a robot on auto pilot. He worked long hours at the shop just so he wouldn't have to be at home alone. All his waking and sleeping hours were taken up with thoughts of her. No matter what he did, she was there. Only work gave him a reprieve from his torment. He worked himself until he couldn't stand up anymore and then went home and crashed. This had been the extent of his life since the woman he loved walked out of it. He couldn't face the fact that Sarah may be right. He had to hold on to his hope that Shea would come back to him.

He decided to take the weekend off and go hiking in the mountains like he and Shea used to. The last time he'd gone was with her. It would give him a chance to think about things. Feeling better for his decision, he went upstairs to get his camping gear together before returning to work. It was February and still cold, but nothing could beat being in that crisp cold air. He and Shea used to go hiking regardless of the weather outside.

Eventually Billy knew he would be able to put his life back together, but one thing he was sure about. He would never be able to love another woman as long as he lived.

CHAPTER TEN

Billy leaned against a rock, letting the sun warm his face. The wind was fierce, but under the protection of the sunlit rock he was warm. He opened up his candy bar and sat back to enjoy it. He'd forgotten how much he loved the woods. A brook babbled nearby. Closing his eyes he dreamed he was in an enchanted forest.

Thoughts of Shea brought him back to reality. Picking up his gear he headed toward the other side of the lake. It was still frozen, so he took a short cut across the middle. He trudged up the snow-packed road to the Olson's house, an elderly couple that Shea and Billy had made friends with on their many journeys up the hill. Their cabin was right on the lake, with a canoe they had let Billy and Shea often borrow. They'd camp out on the beach and take the canoe out while the lake was still calm. The water was smooth as glass and you could see fish swimming at the bottom. Billy remembered those tranquil mornings when he and Shea would watch the sunrise over the lake. He sighed. Everything in these mountains reminded him of Shea.

The Olsons loved seeing them, too. Although they were pretty much hermits, they enjoyed the company of the two young lovers. Having no children of their own, they sort of adopted Billy and Shea.

During the winter months the two would take trips up the hill just to see if the Olsons were okay. The town never plowed the road to the cabin. Often the Olsons would be stranded indoors for days. The location of the cabin wasn't too far from Billy's shop, so it was a simple matter to park the car down the hill and hike up.

Billy climbed up to the house and stared in disbelief at the for sale sign in the window. Quickly, he stepped onto the porch to pound on the door. Cedric Olson peered out from behind the big oak door, surprised to see a visitor.

"Oh, Billy!" he exclaimed in his soft Irish accent. "What a wonderful surprise. Come on in."

Billy stepped past him into the warmth of the kitchen, taking in the odor of fresh baked banana bread.

"So what ye doin' in this neck of the woods? Thought ye forgot about us, here."

Billy bowed his head. "Yeah, I know," he murmured. "There's been a lot of changes since this summer."

"Ah, yes. Shea went off to college, did she?"

"I don't know," he muttered under his breath.

Cedric leaned in closer. "What's that?"

Ruth came up, hitting her husband in the arm. She held her arms out to hug Billy. "It's great to see you. Come and sit down." As she passed Cedric, she whispered, "I don't think he wants to talk about it." Heading for the kitchen, she smiled at Billy. "Would you like some tea and bread?"

She returned with the bread and a cup and saucer. She smiled sweetly as she helped Billy remove his backpack.

Cedric joined him at the table. "You out camping in this weather?" he commented, surprised.

"Just a day trip," answered Billy.

"Kinda like the mailman, eh? Rain, sleet, snow...."

Cedric and Ruth came from Ireland but had been in the States for most of their lives. They had lost some of their accent, but every once in a while it crept out. They took a liking to Shea the minute they found out her great grandparents still lived there and she was named after them, without the 'O'.

Billy and Shea had often shared with them their dream to travel to Ireland and meet Shea's relatives. It saddened Billy greatly to think now they would never get the chance.

Ruth set a big bowl of her home-churned butter in front of Billy. They talked about his shop and their house and farm. The Olsons had a small barn across the little dirt road driveway, with cows, chickens, and of course, the horses.

Billy tried to wait a few moments for the right time but could hold back no longer. He had to know. "Why is that for sale sign in your window?" he demanded.

Now it was Cedric's turn to bow his head. "Oh, me lad," he

89

groaned. "Ruth and I hoped we'd never have to come to this point, but this winter's been brutal."

Billy understood. He knew it would happen sometime. After all, the Olson's had to be in their seventies.

"Why, last week I could barely get into the barn to feed the animals there was so much snow," continued Cedric.

"Why didn't you call me?" Billy scolded. "You know I'm always here to help." He knew they were too proud to ask for help, but it didn't stop him from offering.

"Don't worry yourself, young Billy. It's been a long time coming. We've been thinking of selling for about the last year, just can't seem to find anyone who wants to live up here. Plus we still haven't been able to sell the animals. We don't want to leave 'em, ye know."

Billy nodded. He'd seen how well they cared for their animals, like part of the family. The farm was all the Olsons had. Billy looked around the cabin he had come to know so well.

"Can I have some time to think about this?" he asked.

"Think about what?" Cedric looked at him. "You don't mean you'd consider buying this place?" Billy smiled. Cedric looked at his wife. "I told you we should have called him first. You were the first person we thought of, Billy, but can you afford it?"

Ruth reached out and slapped him. "That's rude, Cedric."

"No, Ruth," interrupted Billy. "He's got a right to know if I'm able to pay the mortgage, and yes, Cedric I can afford it. Part of the reason I haven't been up is I've taken over the shop for my dad. He's paying me a nice salary. It's just qualifying for a loan. I've never bought a big purchase like a house before, but I'm sure my dad will help."

Ruth and Cedric joined each other in an impromptu dance around the dining room. "Billy, you don't know how happy this makes us knowing the house is going to someone we consider a son. If you aren't able to buy it right away, don't worry. We'll work something out."

"Oh, and I'll keep the animals. I wouldn't want to disturb their environment."

They shook hands on the deal and Billy left. Cedric was right, it was definitely too cold to do any camping this weekend. He was certainly glad he stopped to visit, he'd always loved the house. It was in a perfect location: a lake at your front door, rolling meadows in the back, yet plenty of trees to give it that mountain feel.

◆　　◆　　◆

Louise Peabody had been a God-send. Shea had been pretty tired after the birth, and it had been wonderful having someone who went to the crib the minute the baby cried. Shea mostly rested, although she did spend plenty of time with her new son. She told him all sorts of stories about his grandparents. She also read the necessities, like <u>Goldie Locks and the Three Bears</u> and <u>Mother Goose</u>. She'd heard it was good to read to them when they were infants, it helped them understand the written language better. She'd also learned babies that are read to, learn to read faster than other children. Besides she loved just spending time with him.

Shea knew all too soon, the time she had with Ben would be cut short. She'd already decided to start the Spring semester. With a child to provide for, she felt she needed to get finished with school as quickly as possible so she could get a decent paying career going.

How lucky she had been, her parents had left her with enough to live on while she attended college. They certainly hadn't thought she would be supporting a baby at this stage of the game, and neither had she. Still, it was enough, and now that she was eighteen, the money was all hers.

Lifting her eyes to the ceiling, she whispered, "Did you ever imagine?" She often spoke to her parents, who she felt watched over her. "He sure is beautiful. I think he looks a little like both of you." She blew a kiss skyward. "Your grandparents were the best, little buddy. I only wish they could have met you."

She studied Ben for a long time. He did look like her side of the family, which she was glad about. Although his hair was dark, the doctor told her that babies born with darker hair often get lighter with age. But Ben was definitely a Parks no matter the color of his hair.

Ben stirred, letting a little gas pass. His mom grinned. "Why, you even have the Parks' plumbing!" She settled further back in the rocker and placed Ben upon her shoulder, softly tapping his back while she sang a lullaby her mom had taught her. Ben put a bunched up little fist close to his mouth and began sucking on it. She heard him let out a little burp before he drifted off back into slumber.

CHAPTER ELEVEN

As soon as the buzzer sounded, the students bounded from their seats and raced out of the room. Shea finished putting her books together, grabbing her purse from the back of the chair. There were still a few students cleaning up their areas, but for the most part the room was empty.

"Ms. Parks, can I see you for a moment?"

Startled, Shea looked up at her instructor, wondering if she were in trouble. She gathered up her books. "Be right there, Grey!" Grey was his last name but he insisted people use it as his first. Shea glanced over her shoulder at three girls huddled around talking at the back of the class. They were pointing and whispering at her and the teacher. All the girls on campus thought Grey was a 'babe.' It was common speculation that he dated many of his female students.

Who wouldn't want to date him? She thought. After all, he was drop-dead gorgeous, with his wavy brown hair, and green-blue eyes that looked right into your heart.

Shea never took much notice of the men on campus. She was too busy during the day with school, and at home she was either studying or taking care of Ben. Nor did she have time for the parties everyone raved about.

The three gossips made their way from the room, leaving Shea and Grey alone. Shea could feel a shiver travel through her body that she couldn't explain as she walked slowly up to Grey's desk. She watched as he took her project out from under his desk and lay it out in between the two of them. Shea suddenly realized the feelings she had were ones of dread. He had handed back everyone's project except hers.

"Did you do this by yourself?" Grey asked.

Shea switched her books from on side of her hips to the other. She nodded cautiously.

"This is quite remarkable. What's your degree in?"

Shea shrugged. "I don't quite know yet, I haven't fully decided. I'm leaning toward business but not sure what area yet."

"Have you considered a career in marketing?"

"I've thought about it. I took this class as an elective but I'm really enjoying it."

"By the looks of this story board, it likes you, too. I've never seen such creativity in a student of mine. Unfortunately, most people who take this class, do it because they think it's an easy "A". Where did you get the idea for a children's clothing store? It's brilliant."

Shea let out a small laugh. "It comes from experience, I guess. I had a son about five months ago, and...."

"Oh, I didn't realize you were married. I'm sorry, I was going to suggest...."

"I'm not married, Mr. Grey," interrupted Shea. "And I certainly don't need a date, especially right now," she retorted. Spinning on her heel she started for the door.

"I wasn't going to ask you for a date," he sputtered with laughter.

Shea turned back in confusion.

"I was going to ask if you'd like a job. I guess I figured if you were married, your husband might not like you both working and going to school, especially since you have a young child at home. We could use your talent at my office."

Shea walked back to him, her eyes shining. "A job?" she asked excitedly. She had figured she'd have to finish school before she could look for work.

Grey smiled at her enthusiasm. "That got your attention. I guess my reputation precedes me here. I just want you to know I didn't make up the rumors and I certainly don't live up to them. I wish I were so lucky."

Shea laughed at what could have been an embarrassing moment. She really liked Grey. He was an excellent instructor with a warm sense of humor. She found it easy to talk to him as he made her feel at ease.

"Here's the deal," he said, perching on the edge of his desk. "My boss, the company owner, asked me to find him a 'girl Friday.' Now, it's not much but it can work into a lot more. It's part time and he'll work around your schedule here."

Shea was thrilled until she remembered Ben. With a heavy heart, she sighed. "I'm really grateful you asked me, but I'm going to have to decline. With school and study time, I hardly get to see my son as it is. I really could have used this job, too."

Grey got up and patted her shoulder. "Why don't you think about it? This really is a great opportunity with plenty of hands-on experience. It could even be a great career move." With a smile he packed up his briefcase and walked out of the room.

Shea slumped into a seat, thinking about his offer. She'd been so wrapped up in the offer she'd forgotten to ask what kind of company it was.

When she got home, Aunt Vicki was in the kitchen feeding Ben his cereal. His little hands and feet moved rapidly in all directions when he saw his mother. At six months, he was starting to show his enormous size. He ate heartily, loved to play and was very active. He'd already started to crawl, which kept Vicki busy during the day chasing after him.

When he saw his mom, he squealed and blew a raspberry. Cereal flew all over the kitchen, making both Shea and Vicki laugh.

Picking him up, Shea twirled the giggling baby around. "How's my big boy?" He laughed hysterically. Then he grabbed her necklace and put it in his mouth.

"You best be careful doing that," scolded Vicki, "you're liable to be wearing his dinner."

Shea grinned and sat down at the table. "Won't be the first time, huh, Ben?" She tickled him.

"You're late today," noted Vicki.

Shea took the necklace off and gave it to Ben. He promptly shook the beads over his head. Shea sighed. "Aunt Vic, I got a problem I need help with."

"What is it, hon?" Vicki licked the last of the cereal off her knuckle.

"Well, it's not really a problem, but there's this instructor at

95

school who really likes my work. And, well, he offered me a job. He said his boss is looking for a 'girl Friday.'"

"And you want to take it." It was more a remark than question. "I thought you were going to concentrate on your studies?"

"I am, that's just it. I think I've decided what I want to get my degree in, and this guy is offering me a job in that field. It would be a foot in the door and could lead to a good career."

Vicki thought for a long while. "It could be pretty lucrative. What about Ben?"

"That's the problem. With all the units I'm taking, if I took the job I'm afraid I'd never see him."

"I understand. I hated leaving my kids even when I knew they'd be in school, but you have to work, too. It's hard being a single mom. You're always afraid your kid will resent you for not being around, yet you have to work to support them. It's not an easy decision, but if you want to take the job, I'm sure we can work something out for baby-sitting."

Mrs. Peabody had been gone for a couple of months now, and it seemed Shea needed her more now than ever. Aunt Vicki had been gracious enough to watch Ben during the day while Shea was in class, but Shea didn't want to take advantage of her. She'd done so much for her already.

"I think you ought to take it," advised Vicki firmly. "Ted's wife, Peg, runs a day-care in her house. If I need to, I'm sure we can take him there. This sounds like too good an opportunity to pass up. How many people do you know that have a job in the field they like before they even graduate from college?"

The two sat back and talked further about it. Ben was still shaking the beads around in his fist. Shea rubbed the blond curls that were beginning to replace the dark hair he was born with.

Shea could see Vicki was excited for her, but she secretly wondered if the excitement was about being able to spend more time alone with Ben. Vicki adored her grand-nephew. She was very good with him, but never overstepped her bounds with Shea. Shea also appreciated the fact her aunt always let her take over when she got home. She never told her what to do with her son and she followed Shea's orders when she was gone.

96

Shea felt a rush of relief wash over her. She knew in her heart this was an offer she shouldn't pass up. She would tell Mr. Grey first thing in the morning.

◆　　　◆　　　◆

The job was everything she'd hoped for. She took her classes in the morning and then worked until five o'clock. She was still home early enough to play with Ben and give him his bath before bed, and spent most of the evenings and weekends studying. But she'd take what she called 'Ben breaks,' where she'd stop her studying long enough to catch a hug or giggle with him.

On weekends, Ted and Peg took Ben to give Vicki a break. They loved spending time with him, treating him like their own son.

Shea couldn't believe all the support she was getting from her new family. They had all rallied around when they found out she was pregnant. When the baby arrived, they even pitched in to help with clothes and furniture.

Shea looked at her watch. It was nine o'clock. She tried for a while to resist the urge to call, but she missed Ben. Finally it got the best of her. Hopping onto the bed she dialed Ted's number. It rang a few times before Peg finally picked up.

"Hi, Shea," she said before Shea spoke.

"How'd you know it was me?" laughed Shea. "How's he doing?"

"Sleeping like a little angel. He's such a little doll. How's school going?"

"Good, thanks. And I'm learning a lot at my new job. Well I won't keep you, give Ben a kiss for me."

"I will. You study hard and I'll talk to you tomorrow."

Shea hung up and trudged back to her desk. She stared down at the pages as if they were blank. She'd had enough studying for one night. Slamming the books closed, she stacked them in the corner and went downstairs to the den.

Vicki was asleep in the chair so she quietly sprawled out on the couch. She played with the remote until she found a movie to watch. It was nice relaxing for a change. She let her aunt be, thankful for a few minutes to herself.

$\mathscr{C}$HAPTER TWELVE

Billy watched the sun slip behind the trees. Basset, his yellow lab, poked his nose up under Billy's hand, looking for an ear scratch.

"Watcha doin', ol' boy?" He reached over and rubbed the dog's head. It was late May. The days were pretty warm, but the nights still cool. Billy pulled his jacket around him, aware of the fact the warming sun was fast disappearing.

He pulled another beer out of the ice chest and popped the tab. Taking a long swallow, he looked at his watch.

"Late!" he mumbled. He put another log on the fire, pushing the cinders around with the toe of his boot until the new log fell into the pit and caught fire.

Basset jumped up and ran around barking. When Billy caught on he headed up the bank toward the house. "Settle down boy, we don't want to scare him away."

He watched as the old Dodge Diplomat pulled to the side of the dirt drive and stopped. An older man got out and walked toward him. Billy hesitated for a moment, thinking there had been some mistake. How could this elderly man be a detective? "Can I help you?" he asked.

The man moved his short, slightly bent figure toward Billy. "Sam Wallace," he announced, holding out his hand. He looked around him in awe. "This place is great. Lived here long?"

"About four years." Billy studied the man the detective agency had sent over. Sam's long, gray hair was pulled back in a ponytail, and he had a bandanna wrapped around his head like something out of the sixties. He wore a jean jacket with jeans worn so thin in parts, Billy could see his skin through them. He was having second thoughts about hiring such a person.

"I'm Billy," he said finally, staring at the elderly man. He led him back down the path to the lake.

"I'm a friend of your attorney," said Sam. "He said you needed help."

Billy nodded as he ushered him through the trees and down the path to the stony beach. He put another log and some lighter fluid on the smoldering fire and brought it to life again.

"Is this all yours?" asked Sam, turning in a circle to take another look at the spectacular view. It was pretty dark but the moon was bright.

"Yep," answered Billy, "bought it from some friends of mine. Pretty great, huh?" Sam nodded and sat down in the chair Billy offered him.

"Would you like a beer, Mr. Wallace?"

"Nope, don't touch the stuff. Got me in a lot of trouble few years ago."

Billy quickly put his half empty can behind the cooler, then offered him a coke, which he took. Billy sat in the chair next to him and tapped the logs with his boot to keep the flames going.

"So, Phil tells me you're the best?"

Sam shook his head. "Don't know if I'm the best. Just know I've been at it a long time."

"Tell me about some of the cases you've handled."

"Not much to tell. I worked for the City of Albany for most of my career. After I retired, I kept getting called by them so I decided to work for them doing temporary jobs. Don't do much now but small cases like yourself, and of course favors to friends." He took a slug of coke. "Phil says you think someone's been stealing money from your company?"

"I don't think, Mr. Wallace. I know. I even know who it is. What I need you to do is prove I'm right."

"Who is it?"

"It's my brother, sir."

"Hmmm. I don't want to go getting messed up in no family squabble."

"I can guarantee this is no family squabble. See, my dad is very ill right now. I don't want to worry or involve him in this until I have proof that it's actually happening. If you work for me and find

99

out my brother isn't involved in any way I'll drop the whole thing. Is it a deal?"

Sam thought for a moment. "These family things can get pretty messy. Fella can get hurt if he ain't careful."

Billy nodded. The two men shook on the deal and talked about strategy. Sam was to work in the company to get an idea of the business. He knew from experience there was more than one way to skin a cat, and even more ways to extract money from a company. Each way held its own laws of prosecution. Sam always went for the whole kit and caboodle when he went for a conviction. Get as much dirt on the suspect as possible. That way when they were finally arrested, there was more than one charge to be considered. Never, he told himself, leave any leeway for the attorney to get his client off.

Billy was willing to cooperate completely. Any doubts he had when he met Sam vanished after talking with him. His father had given him permission to run the company as he saw fit. When Billy first noticed something was wrong, he talked it over with his dad. Jake made it very clear it was Billy's problem and he should deal with it himself. After four years of regular decline in profits, Billy decided to take his father's advice and fix the situation. He had worried about what his dad would say when he was told it might be Kevin behind the whole scheme. What he finally realized was, that his dad didn't want to know the particulars. Billy then felt comfortable facing the situation. He'd given his brother enough chances to turn himself around, and take responsibility. Billy suspected Kevin might even be trying to take over the company in some way. But whatever he was doing, Sam Wallace would find out and put a stop to it.

After Sam left, Billy sat back and relaxed for the first time in months. The problem had really begun taking its toll on both him and the company in more ways than he cared to think about. He'd already started laying people off to cut back on expenses. Although he was able to expand the business into other areas, there was still a substantial loss. Farm equipment wasn't selling like it used to.

Billy swallowed the last of the beer and put the empty can in the cooler. Kicking dirt to extinguish the fire, he made his way back to the house, followed by Basset. He looked around the room, thinking about Shea as he did every night. He had never gotten over her leaving. This house was supposed to be for both of them. He knew as long as he lived there would never be another woman for him. Shea was it and no one could take her place. He sighed as he got ready for bed, feeling old before his time. His heart felt like lead.

CHAPTER THIRTEEN

It was mid May. The sun shone brightly as Shea finally walked across the stage to receive her diploma. A lot had happened since she'd started school. Ben had grown up so quickly, now sporting her platinum, blonde curls. He'd just turned four and was developing quite a personality. He was so active, Shea found it difficult to keep up with him.

She still worked for Abbott enterprises, and now having obtained her degree, Henry had a special project planned for Shea to take over. He teased her, refusing to tell her about it until she'd actually graduated. He said he wanted her to concentrate on her studies, but she suspected he liked keeping her in suspense. Shea could hardly wait for Monday so she could find out what her first big project and responsibility was going to be. She'd already been in charge of several projects in the office, but this one promised to launch her career in the right direction.

In January of that year, Vicki had suffered a large stroke, leaving her totally incapacitated. After she'd gotten out of the hospital, she'd summoned the family together to tell them of her decision to live in a nursing home. She and her late husband owned a few of them as well as being on the hospital board. She insisted on going somewhere where she could be cared for twenty-four hours a day. At first the family balked at the suggestion, but once she convinced them it was what she preferred, they gave in.

The house was sold and Ted and Peg auctioned off most of the furniture. What was left they split up between themselves. Shea, had bought a small cottage on the beach where she and Ben went to live. She loved the little house and with the furniture from her aunt's house, along with some pieces she found at garage sales, she was able to make a comfortable home.

They visited Vicki regularly, and today would be no different. After Shea's ceremony, she, Grey and Ben headed over to the nursing home. Grey and Shea had become good friends since she started working for Henry Abbott. After she finished his class, he even hinted about them going out together. Shea explained it was out of the question, but they still remained close. They talked often, Shea even telling him bits and pieces about her past and how she ended up in Florida. He was good with Ben and they often did things together.

Ted and Peg couldn't make the graduation ceremony. It bugged Shea a little because they didn't offer an excuse, just that they wouldn't be attending. She felt hurt, but refused to let it ruin her day.

Grey pulled into the lot of Aunt Vicki's nursing home, parking up close to the front entrance.

"Hey, isn't that Ted and Peg's car?" demanded Shea.

Grey shrugged, concentrating on parking. "I don't think so."

Shea was certain it was. She became concerned in case something had happened to Vicki. Clambering out of the car, she dashed up to the door, followed by Grey carrying Ben. It wasn't until she got to the front door that she saw the banner. *'Congratulations Shea!'* She gaped at Grey in delight. Inside the nursing home she found some of the residents lined up, holding balloons. They applauded as she walked by. With a huge smile, she thanked them, allowing Ben to take the balloons, and play with them.

It wasn't until she got to the dining room she saw the extent of what was happening. There were tables of food everywhere and a huge cake, iced with the word, 'congratulations'. Ted sneaked up behind her and grabbed her in a bear hug. "Congratulations, sweetie."

Shea looked around in a daze at all the people and decorations. Even Mr. Abbott was there with his wife. She spotted Vicki, propped up in her bed in the corner of the dining room. Going to her, Shea bent down to hug her. "You did all this didn't you?" she scolded.

Vicki smiled demurely. "Well, I couldn't make it to your graduation, but wanted to be a part of it, so this is it! We're always happy to have an excuse for a party."

Shea threw her head back and laughed. "You're too much." She looked at Ted and Peg, who stood smiling. "I suppose this why you couldn't make it to my graduation?"

They both nodded and laughed. Ben came toddling over to Vicki's bed. "Grandma, look at all the balloons I have!" He climbed up next to her.

With her one good arm, she pulled him close and kissed him. "Are you having fun, Ben?"

He nodded, jumping back down off the bed. Peg had set up a small table for him out of one of the coffee tables where she had set down a fruit drink and plates piled with his favorite foods. Everyone made a line around the buffet table and started filling their plates. Ted fixed a plate and brought it to his mom. A nurse waited to help her eat.

Shea got herself a glass of punch, then rapped the table. "Everyone, if I can have your attention for just a moment! I'd like to thank each and every one of you for your part in making my party so special. I can't think of a better group of people to celebrate with. You've all meant so much to me over the past few months and you're all such a great group of friends to my aunt. I especially want to thank Ted and Peg, even though they were very sneaky."

Small giggles sailed through the room. Then with tears in her eyes she thanked Vicki for all the support and love she'd given her over the past years since she'd come to live in Florida. After the speech and with everyone still watching, she went over and hugged her aunt the tightest she ever had.

"I love you so much, Aunt Vicki. Without you I would have none of this. I could never thank you near enough for the support and love you've given me."

Vicki's eyes shone. "Getting your degree is thanks enough. I'm so proud of you. When you came here under the situation you did, you just plowed through your problems and dealt with them. After everything you've been through, you never lost your sense of self. My dear, you have overcome many odds, you're going to do great things."

They gazed at each other with love and respect. They both felt as strong about what had happened. They knew it was because of each other's support that they both made it through the toughest times of their lives. Vicki lost her sister, and Shea her mom and dad. Then the rape. But it was time to put it all far behind and look ahead to the future. Shea fought the rising tears.

Ben ran over and hugged his mom's leg. "Mommy, why are you crying? Are you sad?"

Shea bent down and picked him up, holding him close. "No, honey. Sometimes people cry when they're happy, too."

"Are you happy, then, Mommy?"

"Yes," she whispered. "Mommy's very happy. And you, my sweet," she took his face in her hand, "you make Mommy happiest of all."

The rest of the day went beautifully. Shea helped Peg and Ted clean up, then made the rounds, saying good-bye to all the residents at the home. Ben had gathered up the balloons, carrying them around, lost behind the big bouquet they made. Grey loaded all Shea's gifts into the car then came back for her and Ben. Aunt Vicki was sleeping, so Shea lightly kissed her forehead and left the card she'd gotten her on the bed next to her.

When they finally got back to Shea's house it was already dark. Ben had fallen asleep in the back seat. Grey switched off the ignition. Turning his head to look at Shea, he reached over and touched her hair. She pulled away instantly. "Grey, please."

Grey slapped his hands on his thighs. "Shea, what is wrong with you? You cringe if I even try to touch you."

Shea sat back against the seat with her arms folded in front of her. "Grey, we've been through this before. I certainly do not cringe when you touch me! This has nothing to do with the rape, I just don't think it's a good idea for us to get involved. We work together, I've told you how I feel."

"Yeah, all too well. Maybe if I quit my job...."

"Don't be silly. Even if you did, there's no guarantee I'd go out with you."

"Then it is the rape isn't it? You know, eventually Shea, you're going to have to learn to trust someone. Not every man is out to hurt you."

Shea thought about that. Really, she wasn't sure she'd ever be able to love any man again. Grey was such a great man, and he loved Ben. But there was a lack of feeling or something Shea couldn't quite put her finger on. Something missing. Tiredly, she got out of the car and pulled the seat up to get Ben out of his car seat.

"So, you don't want to talk about it, is that it?" snapped Grey.

"Not that I don't want to talk about it, Grey. I just don't want to talk about it *now*. It's not a good time, I need to put Ben to bed."

"Shea, it's never a good time with you. That's just what I mean, you always find an excuse to avoid the issue. Are you going to do that for the rest of your life?" His voice was harsh.

"Maybe I am!" she countered. "It's none of your business anyway." Slamming the car door, she headed for the house.

Grey got out and followed her. "Yeah, well, you can't keep avoiding the issue forever. Eventually it's going to catch up with to you."

Shea ignored him and kept walking. Unlocking the door, she headed for Ben's room. She laid him on the bed and began undressing him with Grey hovering behind her. Shea got Ben's clothes off and tucked him in, trying to ignore Grey. Up to now she hadn't had to deal with the issue of relationships. She'd put them all off, saying it interfered with school. Now it was time to face the music.

"Look, I'm sorry I said all that," he said softly, as they moved quietly from Ben's room. "It's just that...."

The phone rang, interrupting him. Relieved, Shea moved to answer it. A moment later, she dropped the receiver as her legs buckled under her. "No!" she cried out.

Grey went to her. "What is it, Shea?"

Shea huddled against the wall, covering her face. "Oh God, no..." she sobbed. "It's Aunt Vicki. She just died."

Grey sat down on the floor beside her, rubbing her back. "I'm so sorry."

Shea sat for what seemed like hours, clinging to Grey. How comforting it felt to be held. She wished she loved Grey. He was so kind and gentle, but she just didn't have the feelings she should.

Shea sobbed until she was exhausted. She owed so much to Aunt Vicki. How could she go on with out her? And what would she tell Ben? She was like a grandmother to him.

Grey held her until she fell asleep in his arms. Gently, he carried her to the couch and laid her down. He covered her, stooping to kiss her forehead, but stopped mid-stream. He watched her for a minute before he turned to leave. Locking the house behind him, he went to his car.

There he sat for a while thinking about the afternoon. He knew Shea was right in one respect. Office romances often didn't work out, but he had hoped they were different. He also came to the realization that Shea was in a different place from him. She was fresh out of school, just starting her career. He was established, even looking for something different. At work they made a great team, but somehow he knew it would never be more than a work-ing relationship. He decided not to spoil their friendship by pressuring her anymore.

Feeling better that a decision had been made, Grey drove away, glancing at Shea's picture-perfect cottage in his rearview mirror.

◆　　◆　　◆

Shea circled with the tray of hors d'oeuvres again and made sure everyone's drinks were full before she headed back to the kitchen. One of her aunt's friends stopped her, taking the tray from her hands.

"Hey, you shouldn't be working, let me take that. You go talk to your guests."

Shea looked for Ted again, but couldn't find him. He had taken his mother's death very hard. Peg had a constant eye on him, spending so much time comforting him that the funeral arrange-ments fell into Shea's hands. She had offered to host the reception in her tiny house, so Ted could grieve in peace if he needed to.

Aunt Caroline stood in the corner of the dining room, whispering to her husband. Shea tried hard to avoid her, counting the minutes until it was time for her to go. Returning to the kitchen, she checked on the glass situation. As she dried some glasses, she heard a voice behind her that made her hair stand up on the back of her neck.

"I see you've done well for yourself here, Shea." Shea didn't reply, hoping the lack of response would make Caroline go away. "Cute little boy," Caroline commented. "Is he Grey's?"

Shea put the towel down, turning to get the dirty dishes off the counter behind her. "Yes," she lied. She knew from past experience not to feed the gossip mill that was her aunt's forte.

"Grey seems very nice. He told me you two weren't married. That's strange since you have a child together."

Shea bristled, turning back to the sink. "Well, that's our business," she answered coolly. She filled the sink with water and poured the soap in. Ignoring her aunt, she took out her frustration on the dirty dishes, not wanting Caroline to know how much she got to her.

After a moment, Caroline tried another tact. "I must say, Shea, you seem to have gotten over your situation back home, pretty well."

Shea dropped the sponge she was holding and turned to face her aunt. "My situation?" she scoffed in contempt. "You mean the rape. Why don't you call it what it was, Aunt Caroline?" Her fury grew. "I was *raped!*" she yelled, advancing on her aunt. "You can't say what it really was, can you?" She backed her aunt into the corner.

Ted hurried into the kitchen. He put his arm around Shea to lead her away. Shea resisted, still facing Caroline. "You know it was rape, you bitch and you did nothing...."

"Shh, come on now." Ted managed to get her through the crowd that had gathered to watch the commotion. They went to Shea's room, followed by Grey. Allowing Grey to take over, he returned to the kitchen to finish off Caroline.

"I think you should go now," he said sternly. "The party's almost over and people are leaving, anyway."

Caroline huffed, but got her purse and sweater. Her husband, John, just followed her out with a dazed look on his face.

CHAPTER FOURTEEN

Shea thumbed through the mail on her desk. Henry walked by her office then stopped, popping his head round the door.

"I didn't expect you back so soon!" He made his way into her office. "You could've taken more time, you know. It's only been ten days."

Shea nodded. "I know, and thanks, but I can't stay home any longer. All I do is think. I'm ready to get back to work. So, what have you got for me?"

Henry looked through the files in his hand and handed her one. "Can you look at this for me?" he asked cautiously.

Shea opened the file and sighed. "I can do this for you, but I'm ready to get back to what I was doing before I left. As I recall...." she hesitated, getting up from her seat. "You said you wanted to talk to me first thing Monday morning."

Henry didn't meet her eyes. "Yes, I did Shea, but I want you to be absolutely sure you're ready to work. That was a tough blow you suffered. I know how close you were to your aunt."

"I know, Mr. Abbott, but I need to work. It's the best therapy for me to deal with grief. I'm fine, really and I can handle anything you give me."

She sat down, putting the file down in front of her. "I'll have this done by this afternoon."

"Okay." He sat in the chair opposite. "There is something I wanted to talk to you about... you know you and Grey are my strongest workers. You two work real well together."

Shea nodded. "So you need us to work on something?" She wondered if it was such a good idea, considering their conversation the week before. He had called a few times to see if she was all right, but never brought the subject up again. She wasn't sure how he felt.

"Not really," said Henry. "See, you two are so good I figured you'd both do just as well on your own projects."

Shea smiled in delight. "Really, you want to give me my own project?"

Henry grinned and nodded. "Actually it's a pretty big project, but I want to be sure you can handle it. It's going to take a lot of hard work and concentration from you."

Shea grinned. "Henry, I won't let you down. I've been wanting to get on with my career for a long time, now. I promise I'll give you whatever it takes."

"I know that, Shea, but that's not all of it." She looked at him, confused. Henry rubbed his hands together. "It's not around here. As a matter of fact it isn't even in this state." He paused. "It's a great opportunity, though. Think about it before you give me an answer."

Shea considered for a moment. "You mean I'll have to relocate?"

Henry nodded. "Yes, but don't worry. It's in a place you know well. I looked over your application when you came here and found out you were from the upstate New York area. When I got this proposition I immediately thought of you. You're perfect: you know the area, you know what you're doing."

Shea looked at him in shock. She had never told him the reason she came to Florida in the first place, so he had no idea what this meant to her. She'd wanted to go back and visit her friends many times but could never summon the courage. When she found out Billy had gotten married, she'd lost all desire to ever go back there again. There was nothing to go back to.

Henry got up and leaned across the desk. "Shea, please think about it. It's a great job opportunity. There'll be a big raise and many benefits involved."

After he left Shea tried to calm her hammering heart. What was she going to do? This was possibly the biggest promotion of her life! Was she going to have to turn it down, because she still didn't think she was ready to go back there, yet?

She knew she could stay in this office, and work smaller jobs, but she was worth so much more. This might be her only chance. Getting up she hurried down the hall to Grey's office.

"Coffee Shop, now!" she called.

Grey caught up to her in the hall. "What the hell?"

She walked with her arms crossed looking down at the floor. Grey could tell she had something important on her mind. When they got down to the cafe, Shea slid into a booth, leaning her chin on her hands.

"Well, I got my assignment," she announced dryly.

The waitress came by and Grey ordered two coffees. "Yeah, me too."

"But Grey, he wants me to go to Albany. Says as I'm from there and know the area it's a great opportunity."

He looked at her, stunned. "Albany, huh? What are you going to do?"

Shea shook her head. "I don't know." Her lower lip trembled. Grey took a handkerchief from his pocket and handed it to her. "What should I do? I haven't been back there since the rape. I don't know if I can go back."

"Maybe you should try. You'll never know unless you do."

"That place holds so many bad memories."

"You know, Shea, I don't want to be the one to tell you what to do, but you'll be passing up a great opportunity if you don't go. Don't let that rapist run your life, you can't stop living because of him. If you don't take this job, you're allowing that creep jurisdiction over your life."

Shea dabbed at her eyes with the handkerchief. "You're right, but I'm so afraid of seeing him." She shivered, remembering Kevin's dark eyes.

"Take control of the situation. Look, you know you'll never get in a car with him again. Besides, the dude is most likely long gone. You don't hang around after you do something like that."

Shea smiled and even managed a slight giggle. "You're so wise and wonderful, Grey. I don't know what I'd do without you half the time."

Grey stirred some cream in his coffee and looked at Shea. "Well, you better get used to doing things without me. Henry talked to me this morning, too."

111

"And....?"

"He really gave it to me good, Shea. He wants me to rescue this ailing business in Honolulu."

"Hawaii? You're going to Hawaii? Now, how come I couldn't get a tropical paradise instead of Albany?" Shea reached over and took his hand. "Grey, I'm really happy for you."

He grinned. "Could be worse, I suppose."

"Worse?" she exclaimed. "You've been wanting to get out of Miami forever. Grey, that's just up your alley."

"I know," he agreed with a devious twinkle in his eye.

They both broke out in laughter and settled back to talk about their new ventures. Henry was very insightful and always knew when to give a push to someone. He'd seen Grey's disappointment for some time now, and knew he needed a change. As for Shea, somehow he seemed to think she'd benefit from her new position, too. Although Shea didn't quite see it the same way.

CHAPTER FIFTEEN

It had been a long week. Shea spent most of the days and a lot of her nights getting ready to go to Albany. There was a lot of paper work to mull over before Henry would agree to a deal. He and Shea had talked at length about her upcoming mission. It was going to take a few trips up north before anything was settled permanently. Shea welcomed this arrangement because it would give her a chance to see how she felt being back there again. Henry had given her a welcome option of backing out of the deal at any point.

She dreaded saying good-bye to Ben at the airport. Ted and Peg had promised to take him to Disney World as compensation for her being away. She got teary eyed when she said good-bye to her son. It was the first time she would be away from him for any length of time, and it was killing her. She never wanted work to interfere with raising him, but this was important for both of their futures.

When she cried, Ben asked as he always did, if she was crying happy or sad tears. She seemed almost disappointed that he was not more upset about his mother leaving. He appeared more interested in his trip to Disney World.

Shea said her good-byes and promised to call every day. Ben waved, telling her it would be okay because he was with Uncle Ted. Shea smiled. Even so young, Ben was such a caretaker.

"Don't cry, Mommy," he told her.

Shea giggled silently to herself and wondered at her little miracle, her little man who meant more to her than life itself. She settled into her seat on the plane. All she wanted to do was rest for a while, but she remembered the mass of paperwork waiting in her briefcase. She pulled the case out from under the seat and took a stack out to read.

She was surprised when the stewardess said they'd be landing in ten minutes. Shea put the stack of papers back in her case and collected her belongings around her. The flight had been too short. She could feel her palms moisten with sweat. Shaking her head, she tried to dislodge the bad thoughts consuming her.

"I won't see him, I won't see him," she kept repeating in her mind.

The passengers quickly moved off the plane and into the terminal. Shea found herself carefully searching for her attacker in every face that passed. As none of them looked familiar, she was reassured. She strode swiftly to the baggage claim, checking her watch. She'd wanted to get settled early and give a call to the manager of Rockport Advertising. The company was going belly-up from the owner mismanaging the expenses. The company itself had actually been quite productive until money started going missing, and clients weren't getting what they were promised. Rumor was, the owner got badly into drugs and used company money to support his habit. Henry had gotten wind of it from a foreclosure notice. Always a man for adventure, he called the bank and offered them an easy out. If they decided to go for it, he'd be getting it for a steal.

Shea knew he had already made up his mind, but he still offered her an out if she didn't feel comfortable handling the situation. The company had a couple of lawsuits against it, Shea planned to use that as her excuse if things didn't go well in Albany. She wanted to go by the office and meet Steve, the manager who was holding the company together at the moment. She thought if she could get hold of the record files, she could read through them tonight and be ready with some ideas for their meeting the next day. Her phone conversations with Steve told her she was dealing with a bright, enthusiastic person. He was always very pleasant and ready to help, with a confident air about him. Shea liked that because it showed he wasn't afraid of taking risks. She had detected a slight concern in his voice over his job, but Shea quickly put that fear to rest. He was an asset as the only person who knew the entire workings of the company.

As she took the limo to the hotel, she was pleased to see she was a little ahead of schedule. She liked being prepared, hating it when she was rushed. Henry told her to take her time while she was there. There were a lot of things to consider when making a purchase this big and he wanted no stone left unturned. He even told her to stay longer if she needed. Henry was very thorough which is one reason he was also very successful. Shea realized she'd found a gold mine when she started working for him.

Shea could think of nothing but getting her shoes off when she got to her room. Quickly checking in she hurried down the hall. She kicked her shoes off and sat on the bed, searching through her myriad of phone numbers. She found the one she was looking for, Rockport.

Steve answered in his usual friendly manner. Shea told him she'd just gotten into town and was settled in at the hotel. "Steve, I'd like to talk to you if I could. Before our meeting tomorrow."

Steve grew quiet at the other end. "Ah, sure. Would you like to meet for dinner?"

Shea looked at her watch. It was four thirty. "About six?" she suggested. Steve agreed and was about to hang up. "Oh, one more thing... could you bring me the accounting books you have?" she asked. "I know he didn't keep many, but I'd like to see what you have."

"No problem. I'll meet you in the lobby."

"That sounds great. How about we eat at one of the restaurants here? I still have a lot of work to do on this."

"That's fine with me, Ms. Parks. I also have a couple of documents I think you might be interested in. I'll bring them too."

"Thanks that's fine, and Steve? Call me Shea."

"Yes, ma'am."

With a smile, Shea hung up the phone and unpacked her bag. Shea decided on her white linen suit. It was warm out, even by New York standards. The sun hadn't fully set. It hung like a huge magenta ball in the sky. She stood by the window watching it drop slowly behind the mountains in the distance. She knew the direction she was looking in was the Heldeberg's. She remembered a

115

time when she and Billy had raced all the way up the hill just so they could watch the sun set. They made it just in time to see the last small arc of light fade away behind the hill. Sighing, Shea glanced at her watch and got ready for her business dinner.

♦   ♦   ♦

The meeting had been eventful. The more she talked with Steve, the more she liked him. He was easy to work with and had a lot of his own ideas on how to get the company running again. She called Henry to tell him about it as soon as she returned to her room.

Her duty done for the day, she sat back on the bed and tried to read. Not being able to concentrate, she did what she'd been longing to do since she'd arrived.

The phone rang a few times before Ted picked it up. "I knew it was you, already," he laughed into the receiver. "Ben even knew it was you."

Shea gave a slight giggle. "Well, can I talk to him?"

"Sure, just a minute." Ben got on the phone and said hello in a cheery voice that bought tears to Shea's eyes.

"Are you having fun, baby?" she asked.

"Yeah, Mommy we went to Dizzy World, and then tomorrow we're going to Encot Center."

"I think you mean Epcot Center, sweetie."

"Yeah, that's it," he said in his small voice.

"Are you being a good boy?"

Ben pulled the phone away from his ear. "Ted, are I being a good boy, Mommy wants to know?"

"You're being a super boy and it's am, *am* I being a good boy," he corrected.

"Mommy, Ted says I'm being good. How's your bacation?"

Shea laughed. She was always amazed by the things Ben said. He was so grown up. "Mom's bacation is good, but she misses her little boy."

"I'm not little anymore," he informed her before saying his good-byes. Shea hung up, feeling better now she knew he was okay. She was getting tired, so she put the papers away and turned in early. She'd already scheduled a breakfast meeting for the morning and she needed to be fresh to concentrate on the files.

The next morning, the waiter bought their meals while Shea pored over a few articles Steve had bought to show her. It was disappointing to see the damage the former owner had done, some of which Shea knew couldn't be repaired.

Still, it all needed to be looked at to make a decision. This was still one of the few marketing companies in the area, the plans Henry had for it would surely make it the most popular.

Steve ate in a hurry because he had promised to meet a client. Under the circumstances, Shea decided it was better for him to make the meeting alone. They would meet later to discuss what the client wanted. Shea needed this information to help Henry.

He quickly took one last sip of coffee before excusing himself. He tried to leave money but Shea told him it would all be expensed. Apologizing once more, he jetted off in the direction of the door.

Shea took another long sip of coffee and settled back in the sunlight to study the reports. The warmth of the sun almost made it feel like she wasn't working at all.

A voice made her stop what she was doing. Listening for a minute, she was certain she'd heard it before. She slunk lower in her seat trying to remain inconspicuous, gathering her papers together. The voice grew louder as it got closer. They were talking about the plants on the patio and she knew it was him. She looked in the opposite direction, searching for an escape. She decided to stay put, hoping he wouldn't see her. She buried her head deeper into the papers she was reading.

She didn't realize until they were standing almost on top of her that Billy had seen her. He came around the other side of the table to see for sure. Then there they were... those familiar blue eyes she remembered so well.

It took her a moment to catch her breath. She felt like a child who'd just been caught with her hand in a cookie jar. She didn't know what to say. What was there to say anyway? Billy was married and gotten on with his life. Shea, on the other hand felt like she was still wandering around in the dark somewhere. All the feelings she had for Billy flooded back. She knew she shouldn't feel them. She couldn't, Billy was married now. He belonged to someone else, his wife. The words cut into her heart. All the letters she'd written that went unanswered. She now remembered all the times she checked the mailbox, her heart in her throat. Then the crashing feeling as she thumbed through the envelopes, only to find none from him.

Billy stood in front of her, his mouth hanging open. His face had a look of half elation, half confusion. Shea quickly got up and took her jacket from the back of the chair. Feverishly she piled all her papers together and left as fast as her feet would carry her. When she got around the corner she let out a long sigh, embarrassed at the feelings flooding through her. Looking back through at patio, Billy still stood with a look of shock on his face.

Seeing him come to life, Shea took off to her room as fast as she could, with Billy calling after her. She slammed the door and then fell against it trying, furiously to catch her breath. She hadn't been sure what her reaction would be if she ever saw Billy again, but she hadn't expected them to be the same old feelings she had when he was around her. That warm, tingly sensation traveled up her legs again as she thought about his face. Those piercing, blue eyes and tanned features. Even surprised, he looked gorgeous.

She sank to the floor, trying to control the tears that were now streaming down her face. How can I still feel this way? She thought. It's over between us, it has been for five years. She got up to get herself a tissue, then plopped down on the bed to cry. She thought she was over him, but this proved she was wrong. This was why she couldn't love Grey. She knew now she would never be able to love anyone again. It terrified her. She was doomed to spend the rest of her life without love. The one and only man she ever loved now belonged to someone else. How lucky that woman was, lamented Shea.

◆   ◆   ◆

The knock at the door startled her. She sat frozen on the bed, where she had fallen asleep. She wasn't expecting to see Steve until the following morning and no one else knew she was there.

Except Billy. Maybe he'd come to explain himself, but what good would it do now? The damage had already been done.

"Who is it?" she asked shakily.

"It's room service, Ms. Parks." The voice had a definite accent.

"I didn't order anything."

"Yes, I know," answered the voice. "I have a package for you."

Shea figured Steve might have dropped something by the front desk. She wasn't prepared for what she saw when she finally opened the door.

"These arrived for you a short while ago, Ms. Parks," said the bellboy from behind a huge bouquet of flowers.

Shea took the bouquet from him and placed it on the desk. She went to get the bellboy a tip.

"No, don't bother, Ms. Parks. The tip has already been taken care of, too."

Shea looked at him, confused. "Andre, who bought these?"

"I don't know, Ms. Parks. There was just a separate envelope for whoever delivered these to you."

Shea thanked him, turning back to the flowers. She took the small envelope from the center of the bouquet and opened it.

'My dearest Shea. Where has all the time gone? You look wonderful. Please say you'll see me. I've left my number with the manager. I love you, Billy'.

Shea let the card fall to the bed as she covered her mouth. "How can he do this to me?" she wailed. She remembered back to the letter Aunt Vicki had received. She would never forget the night she read that horrible letter from Sarah, telling her of Billy's marriage.

She grabbed the flowers from the desk and flung the door open. She grabbed the young cleaning girl walking down the hall.

"Here." She almost slammed the vase into the girl's hands. "I want you to take these."

"What shall I do with them?" the startled girl asked.

"Take them home, do whatever you want with them. I just don't want to ever see them again!" Running back into the room, she slammed the door behind her.

119

Why would he do this? she asked, throwing herself on the bed. He was married, for God's sake! Had he become like the other men she'd met, his marriage meaning little to him? How could he do such a thing, not only to her but to his wife.

She was startled by the phone ringing and stared at it, afraid to find out who it was. Could Billy really be that callous? Finally, she picked up the receiver and said hello with a terse tone. There was a pause at the other end before Steve spoke.

"Hi, it's Steve. Are you busy?"

A flush of relief ran over Shea and she fell back onto the bed. "Ah, no. What's up?"

"Well, I thought we could meet for dinner and I could tell you about my meeting today."

"That sounds great. To tell you the truth, I need to get out of here for a while."

"Paperwork starting to get to you, huh?"

"You could say that." she said picking the card up from the bed. She crumpled it angrily and threw it in the trashcan.

"Seven okay?"

"Sounds good to me... Shea, everything all right?"

"Yes, fine," she lied.

"I'll meet you in the lobby at seven."

Shea felt good about getting out of her room. She wanted to forget the episode with the flowers as quickly as possible. She started a bath, maybe some reading in the tub would help her forget.

◆　　◆　　◆

When she got back from dinner she checked at the desk for her messages. Seeing that Ted had called, she couldn't wait to talk to Ben. It was the highlight of her evening to talk to him. Henry had called a couple of times, wanting to see how things were going. She would call him in the morning before she left. She still had a few loose ends to tie up before she got on the plane the next afternoon.

She'd almost forgotten what had happened when she saw the note. *'Shea, please talk to me!'* She crumpled up the note in her hand and carried it to the nearest trash can. She put it in with such force she almost sent the can tumbling to the ground. Catching it, she then stomped off to her room to call her son. Talking to him would certainly liven her mood.

"Oh, Ms. Parks!" called the concierge. Shea turned back to the girl at the front desk. "These also came for you. Almost right after the first ones."

Shea went back to the counter. "Ms. Smith," she said, looking at the tag the young girl wore, "would you do me a favor?" The girl nodded cautiously. "Would you please leave strict instructions for all your help, that if any more flowers are delivered, they're to be given away immediately. I do not want any more flowers sent to my room. Do I make myself clear?"

The girl's eyes grew wide, but she nodded politely. "Yes, Ma'am. But Ms. Parks?" Shea turned back to face her. "What are we supposed to do with them?"

Shea pushed them toward the girl. "Do whatever you like with them. Just don't let them get to my room." She turned and stalked off.

◆　　　◆　　　◆

The two weeks in Albany had gone well, except for the minor problems with Billy. Shea had gathered everything she thought she needed to report to Henry about. She even did some preliminary work on the other marketing agencies in the area. None offered the type of progressive marketing plans Henry wanted established there. They were popular in Florida and Shea knew they'd be a big hit in Albany as well. She'd put together a splendid report and was actually excited about seeing the project here get off the ground. Despite the old feelings she still harbored, she found herself looking forward to moving back there and working on the project. She'd taken a few rides while there and enjoyed seeing her old stomping grounds, despite the bad memories. Being in Albany again made her realize this was really her home. She wanted to bring Ben up somewhere away from the big city, Miami was getting so huge and dirty. She thought about leaving Ted and Peg behind, but pushed it from her mind. This was a golden opportunity, she knew it was her only chance if she were to provide a proper upbringing for her son. Besides, he could visit Ted anytime he wanted. It would be a while before they actually moved from Florida, anyway.

Shea sat back and thumbed through a magazine she'd picked up in the airport shop. It was the first time she was able to relax since she'd gotten to New York. She glanced at her watch. They would be announcing boarding any minute. She felt relieved to be going back home at that moment. She didn't know if Billy had tried to get hold of her. After her conversation with the receptionist, it was clear she would take no calls or flowers from him. Still, she was glad to be getting on a plane. She would be away from him for a while and maybe he'd get the hint. She'd be more careful the next time she was in town.

The attendant announced preliminary boarding just as Shea heard her name being called.

"Shea!" Billy was sprinting down the corridor. "I was afraid I'd miss you. The hotel clerk just told me you checked out and the limo had taken you to the airport." His breathing was ragged.

"Billy, what are you doing here?" She pulled her purse over her shoulder and gathered her things.

"I just have to talk to you. When I saw you the other day in the restaurant, my heart stopped...."

Shea could feel the heat soar through her limbs and settle hard in the pit of her stomach. She didn't want to tell him that she'd had the same feelings. The attendant called for the rest of the passengers to board and Shea walked over to stand in line.

"Shea, please just answer me one thing, then I'll go away, I promise."

She looked at him with contempt. Her feelings were a mixture of hurt for him marrying and anger for him trying to talk to her now. Her sensible side told her they had nothing left to say to each other. Everything that had to be said should be told to his wife. *Wife*, the word kept rolling over in her brain. Billy, her one and only true love was a husband, but not hers.

"Billy, I can't. We don't have anything to say to each other. Please just go away." She could feel herself choking up.

"But why? I have to know why you left."

Shea bowed her head, fighting fiercely to hold back the tears struggling to get loose. She turned away from him.

"Shea, please don't ignore me. You owe me at least that."

Owe him! she thought angrily. I owe *him!* He married another woman not even eight months after she left. He never wrote her back. Why doesn't he get it? She wondered.

The attendant announced final boarding and Shea wanted to get on the plane, but her feet wouldn't move. The attendant stood by the door, ripping tickets.

"Billy please," said Shea, "I'm not trying to be rude, but we really don't have anything anymore. I'm sorry, I have a new life and you... you're married."

The attendant gently tried to guide her onto the plane. "Miss, we really do have to leave." She pulled her through the doorway.

"Okay, okay," she turned once more to look at Billy.

"*Married*, Shea?" he yelled through the closing door. Grabbing the door, he flung it back open, fighting against the flight attendant. "I'm not married, Shea. I never have been! You're the only woman I will ever love."

Shea stopped in her tracks. "What?"

Billy slipped his business card into her hand just before the door shut. "Call me!"

CHAPTER SIXTEEN

Billy couldn't get over what Shea had said. It was obvious she had been getting information from back in New Salem, but who told her he was married? That was a rumor even he hadn't heard yet. He knew how things circulated, having heard a few things about Shea. He ignored them, knowing they were all false. Even if Shea's disappearance was unexplainable, he knew she couldn't be guilty of some of the rumors he'd heard.

"Billy? Billy!" He heard the voice and turned to look at Sam.

They'd been looking over the accounting records for the shop. "I'm sorry, Sam. I've got something on my mind."

"I'll say. Is she pretty?" Sam asked with a grin.

"The most beautiful woman you've ever seen. It's the strangest thing, a girl I went out with in high school showed up. We were supposed to get married, then one night she disappears. I haven't seen her for five years. I tried getting in touch with her, but could never find her. There's a lot more to the story, but anyway, it turns out she thought I was married."

"Why don't you see if you can find her? I could help you."

"She got on an airplane but I was able to give her my business card before she left. She thought I was *married*, Sam!" His voice rose, showing his bewilderment. That would explain why he never heard from her. Billy took a sip of his beer, then turned it around on the table getting lost in the reflections of the bottle. "I don't know what to do, Sam. What if she doesn't want to be found?"

Sam sat back in his chair. "That's a tough one. How much do you love her?"

Billy took another swig of beer, emptying the bottle. "More than ever, I'm realizing. I thought I'd gotten over her. I mean, with the shop problems and my dad being sick, I really haven't had much time to think about it, but... when I saw her it was like she was just there yesterday. The same feelings came back the minute I laid eyes on her. Is it good to love someone that much?"

Sam laid a finger against his cheek, remembering his past loves. "My son, there's no other kind."

"Oh, great. Now what do I do?" demanded Billy. "When she first left, I couldn't sleep or eat... all I did was work. Hell, I even bought this place for her." He tossed his arm around in the air to show off the house he'd carefully decorated for Shea. "We use to visit the folks that lived here. This was always going to be our place."

"Son." Sam took Billy's arm. "There's an old saying. I know it sounds like a cliché, but I have learned to live by it. *'If you love something, let it go. If it comes back, it's yours. If it doesn't, it never was.'* She knows you're not married now, right?" Billy nodded. "Then I'm afraid unless you want to pursue her, which I don't think you do, then all you can do is wait."

"Is there anything to make the waiting easier?" Billy threw away one bottle and got another from the fridge.

"No." Sam took the bottle from his hand. "And this definitely won't help." He put the beer back in the fridge door, grabbing two cokes instead. "Now, let's get on with these accounts."

◆　　◆　　◆

Shea sat across from Henry, her hands clasped together in her lap. She patiently waited while he pored over the pages of documents she had collected in Albany. He nodded approvingly at some, groaning at others. Shea wondered what he was thinking.

If she was surprised to find out Billy wasn't married, she was even more astounded at the feelings erupting inside of her. She actually found herself hoping Henry would buy the company... not just to help her career, but because she really wanted to go back to the Albany area. She was looking forward to her next trip there.

"Hmmm," muttered Henry.

"Well, what do you think?" She asked at last.

"So far things seem okay. There are a few problems we need to deal with... I'll tell you what. I need more time to look over these. You did a great job, last week, Shea. Why don't you take the next two days off, spend some time with Ben. Come back on Wednesday when I should have more of an answer for you."

"Thanks, Henry. I'll see you Wednesday, then." Shea felt a rush of relief. He seemed really interested. She had to fight the urge to get her hopes up about going back to Albany. The deal may not work out. Taking a deep breath, she collected her things and left.

She had gotten home so late the night before, she had to leave Ben at Ted's. Gathering her purse, she searched for her keys. This was a nice surprise, she could hardly wait to pick Ben up.

Shea walked out into the balmy air and looked up at the sky. The sun shone brightly, with a cool breeze off the ocean. It could get pretty hot in Florida this time of year, and it was a welcome relief to feel the air this refreshing. She threw her purse and case in the back seat. If she went right home and changed, she could be at Peg's in time to get Ben for lunch.

Ben was so happy to see her. His things were already packed and by the door, as he ran over and threw his little arms around her.

"Hi, Peg. How was Disney World?" she asked as Peg followed.

"Oh, It was wonderful. We had so much fun. Ben, go and get your Mom's gift."

"You got me a present, Ben?"

"Yep!" He ran to the other side of the couch, bursting back into the hall to hand the bag to his mother.

Shea kneeled on the floor to open the gift, while Ben stood beaming. "A coffee mug! Thank you." She gave Ben a big hug. "This is the best present anyone ever gave me, I'll use it every day." She held Ben away from her to look at him. "So, tell me about your trip. Did you take any pictures?"

Ben went to his bag and dug out the film. He gave his mom a small plastic container, holding the lid closed when he handed it to her. "Don't open it Mom, 'cos you'll spose it."

Peg and Shea laughed. They talked for a while longer, then they said good-bye. Once they were in the car, Shea hugged Ben again. "I really missed you," she said, pulling him close. "And guess what, Mommy got you something too. It's at home, but I thought we'd go to McDonald's first. Would you like that?"

126

"Yeah! McDonald's... *all right!*"

Shea set their trays on a table out on the patio. Ben spotted the playground immediately and wanted to play. "Not until you eat," she scolded setting his burger and fries out on a napkin in front of him. "Here's your toy." She pulled out a plastic figure from his Happy Meal, and he played with it while he ate.

Shea wanted to tell Ben about Albany. Henry hadn't confirmed they'd be moving there yet, but she'd never seen him turn down a challenge. She still couldn't believe how he was able to take a failing business and turn it into a success... it was definitely a gift to be admired. No wonder he was a self-made millionaire.

"Mommy?"

Shea looked at Ben, who held his hamburger out toward her. "Can you take the pickles off?" She reached over, grabbing the two tart pickles and slipped them into her mouth.

"Ben, Mommy needs to ask you something. How would you feel about moving?"

"Don't you like our house, Mommy?"

Shea giggled. "Of course, honey. I mean far away."

"Would I get to see Ted and Peg?"

Shea knew leaving his uncle and aunt would be hard. They'd practically become a second set of parents to him.

"Well, you would, but not as much. See, we'd be moving to upstate New York."

"New Ork? Where's that, Mom?"

"It's pronounced York, honey. Ya, ya. Try it again."

"What's in New YaYork?"

Shea laughed at Ben's pronunciation. "Maybe a good job for Mommy. There's lots of snow in the winter."

"What's snow?"

"Well, snow is cold, white stuff that falls from the sky in small flakes, almost like rain, but lighter. It makes a big, white blanket on the ground and you can slide down hills on big long sleighs. You can make snowmen and things. It's lots of fun."

"Cool!"

Shea laughed. "Where did you learn that?"

127

"Ted says it. Can I play now, Mommy?"

"Sure, sweetheart." He ran for the monkey bars.

Picking up the trash and depositing it in the cans provided, Shea sat down on the bench to watch Ben. He was so mature for his age, he was very good company. She relished the idea of being able to spend a two days alone with him.

A drop of rain fell onto her hand. Looking up, she saw some storm clouds that had made their way directly overhead. "Ben, come on. It's starting to rain."

"Just a minute, Mom." He ran over to the slide.

"Listen, young man. I don't want to have to say it again. Now you mind your manners and come over here."

Ben stopped in his tracks and stomped back to his mother. "Why do we always have to go when I'm having fun?"

"It's starting to rain." She grabbed her purse from the table and took Ben's hand, returning to the car. Picking him up she put him in the back seat. "Put your seat belt on."

Ben worked at his belt as Shea tried to pull the top back over the car. She got it in place just in time before the rain started coming down in buckets. She jumped in the front seat, her hair dripping with rain.

Ben started laughing, pulling his knees up to his belly. "Mommy, you look funny."

Shea looked in the mirror at the strands of hair pasted to the side of her face. "Yeah," she smiled. Catching her son's eye in the mirror, she gave him a wink, getting back out of the car. She pulled the seat forward and ordered Ben out of the car.

"But Mommy, it's raining out." His eyes were wide.

"I know, but how can you play in the rain if you're inside the car?"

With a whoop, Ben rushed from the car into the rain. Shea joined him and ran in circles with him, doing a crazy dance in the middle of the parking lot in the downpour.

$\mathscr{C}$HAPTER SEVENTEEN

Shea and Henry worked hard over the next two weeks to get a proposal ready for the bank. He was sending Shea back to Albany to close the deal. She planned to also look around the area for a place to live as well.

She packed for both herself and Ben. She wanted him to see where they were moving, and also decided it would be a good opportunity to take a vacation with her son. She'd missed seeing him during the past two weeks, but things had been so hectic at work. All the last minute details had to be put in order before she could get on the plane. She and Ben both needed time together, and after the meetings in Albany, they were going to drive to the Adirondacks for some fun.

She finished packing Ben's suitcase, then started on hers. She was cleaning out her briefcase when she came upon Billy's business card. Taking it out she looked at it carefully, running her hands over the embossed print. She held onto it for a moment before putting it in her appointment book.

When she finished packing her bag, she gave Ben a bath and tried to put him to bed, but he was so excited about his coming plane flight, he kept getting up. She finally put him on the couch next to her. After five minutes of television, he was out like a light.

Ben loved the plane and the flight attendants doted on him. They even took him up to the cockpit to meet the pilot. He managed to charm just about everyone he met. Shea realized he got that from her. She remembered as a child, always being yelled at for talking to strangers. He was excited about being in the air, often scrambling over his mom's lap to see out the window.

After they ate, Ben promptly fell asleep. The attendant came by and gently pinned a set of wings to his collar. She told Shea how polite Ben had been the whole trip. The exhausted little boy slept all through their final descent from the air.

129

When they finally landed, Shea collected the half-asleep Ben and trudged down the aisle. A kind, woman sitting close by helped carry one of her bags into the terminal. She thanked her and put Ben down, leading him through the airport to the baggage claim. After they collected their bags, it was off to the car rental place. Ben was ecstatic about his new surroundings, checking out everything he came in contact with. It took Shea some doing to keep him at a movable pace. Still, she delighted in hearing his excited comments about everything he saw.

When they got to the hotel, Shea checked them in. Ben stood next to her, and waved at the housekeeper, who made faces at him. Finally she noticed who he was with.

"Ms. Parks, is that you?" asked the young woman.

Shea swung around. "Eve! Hi," she smiled. Shea realized she made quite an impression the last time she stayed there. There weren't many guests who insisted on the staff taking such beautiful flower arrangements home. There had been four by the time she'd left and more after she was gone. The help took turns taking the bouquets home with them. Despite the reason for it, they had felt special walking out with those big bundles of flowers every night.

"Eve, I want you to meet my son, Ben."

"Well, hello Ben." Eve took the boy's hand.

"Shake her hand, hon." Ben put his hand out to meet Eve's.

"Mommy, do you know this lady?"

"Her name's Eve, baby. We don't call people 'lady'," she whispered gently. "I stayed at this hotel the last time I was here."

"We call your mom the 'flower girl'." Shea grinned. "Oh, Ms. Parks, you have no idea the flowers we got here. I had bouquets in my dining room for weeks." The girl behind the counter shot Eve a warning look, and Eve excused herself.

After they finished checking in, Shea got Ben in his swimsuit and they went to the pool. It was four o'clock. There was a nice breeze and the water was lovely and warm. She figured they'd go for a swim, have dinner in their room, and go to bed early. It had been a long day for both of them.

"Mommy, I'm getting cold."

Shea got Ben out of the pool and dried him off. She wrapped the towel around him and carried him back to the room. They passed Eve in the corridor. She smiled at Shea and hurried past. Once in the room, Shea called room service immediately and ordered a light dinner. She then changed Ben into his pajamas as he could barely keep his eyes open. It didn't look like he'd even make it until dinner. She put him in the queen size bed and got changed herself. By the time she walked out of the bathroom, he was fast asleep. Room service arrived, and she took the tray, being sure to give a good tip. With a sigh she settled in with a sandwich and her paperwork.

Lifting a stack of papers, Billy's card fell out. Confused, she picked it up. She distinctly remembered putting the card in her appointment book. She stared at it again, reliving their meeting at the airport. She had to know if he had never been married, did he still love her? She knew she would never be able to break free of him if they didn't at least talk, have some closure. This visit would be as good a time as any, she supposed, taking a deep breath.

"Well, Ben," she whispered softly, "I guess we have to go for a ride tomorrow."

She put the card in her purse and tried to read her papers, but it was difficult to concentrate. Taking out Billy's card out again, she didn't like the way she felt... out of control. It had been a long time, yet still those same feelings rushed back the minute she had seen him. She thought about Sarah's letter that told her Billy was getting married, and wondered if he'd gotten divorced. But he'd said at the airport he had never been married.

She wasn't even sure if seeing him was a good idea. So many things had changed, they were two different people, now. She did want to introduce Ben to him, though. She wondered if she and Billy could be friends, or ever have any kind of relationship at all.

Realizing she wouldn't be able to concentrate, she put her papers back in the briefcase and turned the light off. She lay in the dark for a while, thinking about everything that had happened over the past five years. So much had changed; she'd lost a lot. Yes, she'd gained a beautiful son, but she had lost Billy, the only man she'd ever loved. She'd been robbed of her innocence, and the one thing she was saving for Billy had been brutally ripped from her. She wondered how she would ever be able to cope with all the memories crowding her mind.

◆   ◆   ◆

It was Saturday morning and the sun was already scorching. Shea and Ben sat on the edge of their beds, wolfing down a huge breakfast of scrambled eggs and biscuits. They had both gone to sleep without eating dinner, the tray still next to the bed.

Shea had wanted to get into town early so she could find a proper baby-sitter for Ben. Her meetings were still a few days away, but she'd already checked with the front desk clerk, who highly recommended a lady named Janet Frey. She intended to call her this morning and arrange a visit before committing herself.

"How would you like to go for a ride?" Shea asked Ben.

He didn't looked up from his plate. "Sure, Mommy. Where we going?" He lifted up a massive piece of egg sandwich and shoved the whole thing in his mouth at once, so the corners were sticking out each side.

Shea broke the two chunks off, trying to ease the bulge. "I wish you wouldn't do that. You're going to choke one of these days." She wrapped the pieces in her napkin and put it on her plate. "I thought we'd take a ride out to where Mommy used to live. Would you like that?"

"You lived here? I thought you lived in Miami."

"I do now." For a few more weeks anyway, she added privately. "But I grew up around here."

"Did you live near the airport?"

Shea giggled. "No honey, Mommy lived a little ways from here." She pulled Ben close to her. "We'll take a ride there and I can show you the town. How would you like to see where Mommy went to school?"

"Cool!"

She mussed Ben's hair and pushed him back on the bed, tickling him. "I'll show you cool."

Ben let out a squeal and they both fell back laughing.

The sun was downright blistering hot, the humidity reaching an all time high. Shea was very glad she'd gotten a car with air conditioning. She and Ben cruised along in the comfort of their sedan. Shea pointed out various sights along the way and Ben watched in excitement as they passed a big dairy farm.

Shea found herself on the road where Billy's shop was. She slowed down as she passed, then turned in at the last minute. Without even realizing it, she'd parked the car in a spot close to the front door. The same spot she always parked when she used to visit him there.

"What are we doing here, Mom?" Ben asked, looking out the window.

"I have a friend I want you to meet."

They walked into the building and Shea looked around. The place looked different. A lot bigger than it used to be. They had added on to the back where they sold lawn mowers and other outdoor equipment, and there was a new a show place area. It looked like they included interior plants, there. That's why Billy was at The Turf, that day, she thought to herself. She looked around for Billy but couldn't see him.

She walked to the counter. "Excuse me, I'm looking for Billy."

The young gentleman was very pleasant. He looked quite young, Shea knew he was probably a teenager working for the summer. It was common to see young kids working there. Billy's dad believed in helping teens learn to reach their full potential. He even sponsored scholarships for underprivileged youth.

The young man told her Billy was gone, but would be back later that afternoon. Shea left her name, telling him to let Billy know she was in the same place as last time.

"He'll know what I mean," she assured him, taking a piece of paper and writing her name on it. "It's Shea, like 'Shay'... never mind, just give him this." She handed the note to him. "Come on, honey." She took Ben's hand. "Let's look around."

Kevin flung the door open and shut it again quickly, catching it before it slammed. "Holy shit!" He couldn't believe what he'd seen, standing less than ten feet in front of him. He leaned back against the door, trying to calm his pounding heart. "What is she doing here?"

He ran his sweating palms through his wavy hair, feverishly thinking about what he should do. He opened the door a crack and looked out again. Her back was to him as she looked at some flowers.

Ben had broken away from his mom and turned toward the model of the lawn mower sitting right outside the office door. He stopped to stare up at the man standing in the doorway. Kevin glared down into the little boy's eyes until Ben got spooked, and ran to his mother. Kevin shut the door again and leaned back.

"Mommy! Mommy!" Ben ran to Shea.

"What, honey?" she said, holding the potted flowers she was looking at.

"There was an ugly man looking at me."

Shea glanced back in the direction Ben had come from, but no one was there. Shea knelt down next to Ben. "Sweetie, we don't call people ugly, okay?"

"But Mommy, he was weird. He scared me."

"I'm sure he didn't mean to. Come on, let's get going. We still have a few more stops to make. How would you like some ice cream? I could sure use some. I know the perfect place." She put the pot back down and took Ben's hand.

◆　　◆　　◆

"Sarah, guess what? Shea's back in town, I just saw her out in the shop. With a kid!"

Sarah boggled at the phone. "Are you sure it was her?"

"Positive. Did she tell you she was back?"

"No, but considering the circumstances...."

"What are we going to do?" He fell silent.

Sarah wondered why Kevin was so upset. It had been five years. Things had blown over. Surely Shea wouldn't remember that night. If she did she probably wanted to forget it. "I don't know, Kevin," she said into the receiver, "but we can't keep her from Billy forever. I wouldn't worry about it."

"I think they've already seen each other."

"What makes you say that?" demanded Sarah.

"Shea said something to Jerry about telling Billy she was at the same place."

"She saw you?"

"No, she was talking to one of the stock boys. I overheard."

"Well, I don't think we should do anything," she advised coolly.

"I'm going to do something... and I know exactly what it is."

"Kevin what are you... Kevin?" Sarah held the empty receiver in her hand.

◆   ◆   ◆

Billy walked behind the counter and opened the register. It started spitting out numbers, he watched as they rolled up. Glancing down, he spotted the piece of paper with Shea's name on it. It was her writing! He'd know it anywhere.

Jerry walked up behind him. "Oh, I see you got your note."

"Did you take this?" demanded Billy.

"Yes, sir. She came in earlier, says you can meet her the same place as last time."

"She said that?"

"Yep, said she wants you to call her."

Billy hopped over the counter and ran for the door. "Tell Kevin to close up for me, okay?" he yelled, sprinting out the door.

"Will do," answered the bemused young man to empty air.

Later, Jerry was busy closing when Kevin came out of the office in a tirade.

"Did you close up, last night?" he bellowed, waving a register tape in his hand.

"You closed up with me."

"I swear, I can't take my eyes off you boys for nothin!"

"Wha... what's the problem?"

"Missing money, that's what the problem is, and I know right where to look. Go on, pack your things... you're outta here."

"But...."

"I said out, and don't think my brother won't hear about this. Scram!"

135

Sam Wallace started moving the mop around the floor again, trying to move back behind the wall before Kevin spotted him.

"What are you looking at?" Kevin yelled at him.

Sam shook his head and mumbled something under his breath.

"Don't know why my brother ever hired you in the first place, ya good for nothing. Whoever thought we needed a mop boy anyway. I tell ya, I should be running this company. I'd get rid of half you losers. Go on, you go home, too."

Sam made tracks out the front door, but went around the back and quietly let himself back in. He huddled behind a stack of bagged potting soil and listened. He could hear Kevin on the phone with someone, but couldn't make out what they were saying.

"Damn!" he whispered to himself. He tried to get closer and sent a bag tumbling off the top. Before it even hit the ground he was out the back door, taking cover in a garbage dumpster. Kevin ran out and looked around the empty lot. Sam congratulated himself for having parked in the front lot, out of Kevin's sight.

As Kevin slammed back inside Sam made his way to his car. He left hurriedly, not wanting to be spotted.

◆　　　◆　　　◆

Shea took a sip of her wine and set it back on the table. "Thank you for dinner. You didn't have to pay, you know."

"I wanted to," Billy rejoined, trying not to show how nervous he was. He'd always been able to talk so easily with Shea. Tonight though, it seemed he couldn't find the words. He'd planned what he would say ever since the last time he saw her but now his tongue was caught in his throat, along with his heart. He took another draft from his beer and set it next to his chair.

Ben had practically fallen asleep at the dinner table, and Shea didn't even bother to put him in his pajamas before tucking him in. She sat out on the balcony, looking in at her sleeping son, trying not to let Billy see how terrified she was.

"Your son is cute." He felt a twinge of jealously creep inside him and he wondered who the boy's father was. Shea hadn't explained anything when she introduced them. He yearned to know if the guy was still in her life.

136

"Yeah, he's quite the little man," replied Shea, studying the sleeping Ben. She wasn't sure how to approach the subject. But she knew by the look on Billy's face he was curious. She took another large gulp from her glass and filled it again. She could feel the effects of the alcohol, but kept drinking because it made her more relaxed, and that was what she needed right now. It had been so long since she'd had a drink, it didn't take much. She settled back in her chair and let the wine numb her.

"He doesn't have a father, you know," she finally announced.

Billy just looked at her.

"My son. He was conceived out of rape."

Billy didn't know what to say. "I'm sorry." He tentatively touched her hand.

"It's okay," she shrugged, feeling tears in her eyes. "I've learned to deal with it. It took a long time, but I'm okay now."

"Shea... is that why you left?"

She nodded, biting down on her lip.

"Why didn't you tell me this?"

"I wrote you five letters. When you didn't write back I figured you were too mad at me." She looked up for a moment as if trying to remember something. "Then I got this letter from Sarah, saying you were getting married." She paused. "That letter sent me into labor you know."

They both giggled.

"I wonder where Sara heard I was getting married?"

"You know how the rumor mill is around that town. I'm sure tongues were wagging when I left." She meant it as a question.

"A few. I tried not to listen."

"I realized I couldn't let those people bother me, I had so much else to deal with at the time."

"That's all you should have been worrying about. I just wish you had come to me, I didn't get any of your letters. If only I had, I would have been down there so fast."

"I planned on coming back, you know. I just needed time to think. Then I found out I was pregnant. I needed Aunt Vicki so much I couldn't leave then either. One thing led to another...."

Shea was feeling more and more comfortable. It was almost like when they were going out. She felt herself wanting to open up. "I haven't dated anyone since."

"I can imagine you mustn't trust men too much, anymore."

"I've never found anyone I liked well enough, and you?"

"I'll be honest. I tried, but it just wasn't there. Every time I was with another girl I was dying inside because it wasn't you. Finally I just told her the truth." He smiled. "You still have your long hair."

"You look the same, too."

Billy looked down at himself. They sat in silence for a moment before they both tried to speak at once. Together they laughed.

"Go ahead, Billy."

"I just wondered what bought you back here?"

"I have a job offer. It's actually a company my boss wants me to run. He saw I was from New Salem on my resume, and thought I'd like to come back up here."

"Well, do you?"

"I think so. I'd like to raise Ben out in the country. I have a chance of doing that here."

"Yeah, you can't beat the scenery up here."

"How 'bout you? Where are you living?"

"Are you ready for a shock?" Shea nodded. "I bought the Olson farm."

"You mean the one on the lake?"

"That's the one."

"I can't believe it! I remember we were always going to buy that place."

"Well I bought it."

"What happened to Ruth and Cedric?"

"They went into a retirement community. Ruth died two years ago and Cedric just a few months ago, but I kept in touch with them regularly." Billy could see Shea was getting tired. He finished the last sip of beer and put the mug on the table. "It's getting late. I should be going." He rose from his seat and Shea followed him.

"It was really nice seeing you, Billy." Her voice sounded strained.

It bothered Billy that they acted like two complete strangers.

"I'd like to see you again if I could," he blurted.

"Well, I'm sort of on vacation here with Ben, too. I promised to take him to Story Town tomorrow."

"It's <u>Great Escape</u> now. I love that place."

"Well, would you like to tag along?"

"I wouldn't want to intrude."

"I'd love it if you came with us. Besides, I think Ben is getting a little bored spending so much time with his mother. It will be a nice break for him. Is ten too early?"

Billy laughed. "No, and why don't we make it eight? I'll buy breakfast."

"It's a deal," smiled Shea, opening the door.

They stood there for an awkward moment. Billy leaned forward to kiss her cheek. Shea retracted so hastily, even she was surprised. "I'm sorry," she stammered. "I don't know what came over me."

"No apology necessary." He took her hand and held it in his. "I shouldn't have tried to kiss you like that. I'm sorry." He turned to leave. "Eight?" He smiled back at her.

Shea nodded. "Yes." She went back in the room and closed the door. The tears came almost immediately. What just happened? She wondered. She recoiled from the one man she knew she could trust. Would she ever be able to trust again? With Grey it was easy, she wasn't in love with him, but her feelings ran deep for Billy. Was she so damaged that she couldn't let even Billy get close to her?

Billy got in his truck and slammed his fist on the dash. "Damn!" He cursed himself. "How could I have been so stupid?"

He'd done the one thing he didn't want to do, move too fast. He still wasn't sure how Shea felt about him. He wanted her more than he ever had, but he knew he needed to move slowly. He hoped all wasn't lost tonight. Shea had left him once and he swore he wouldn't let her get away again. He loved her more than life itself.

Shea opened the door to a big bouquet of flowers. "Oh my, look at these!" she exclaimed, taking them from Billy.

"Again, I'm sorry. I can guarantee it won't happen again."

"Don't be silly. You didn't do anything. I guess we'll just have to take things slower, that's all."

"Agreed." He shook her free hand.

Shea arranged the flowers in the ice bucket sitting on the desk. "Ben's still in the tub. I told him he could have a few more minutes to play. I'll go get him."

Billy went to the window and looked out at the mountains off in the distance. "You can see the hill from here."

"Yes, I know. I had the same room last time."

She brought Ben's clothes in to him and searched for his sneakers. She joined Billy at the window.

"Sure is beautiful," he murmured dreamily.

"Yes, very."

"Mom, can you comb my hair?" came Ben's strident little voice.

"Yes, in a sec." Shea looked at Billy and snickered before turning back toward the bathroom.

A few minutes later they both emerged, with Ben fully dressed. "Say hello to Billy," she whispered, leaning over to his ear.

"Hi, Billy. We're going to Dizzy World."

"No, honey, Story Town."

"Great Es... never mind," said Billy.

Shea smiled at him as she collected the knapsack from the bed.

"I hope you're hungry, Ben," said Billy, tapping his shoulder, "we're going where they serve up a man's breakfast. You think you can eat that much?"

"Yeah!" yelled Ben, skipping out the door.

Billy held out his arm and Shea took it, smiling. As they walked through the lobby, Shea called out to Ben who was running quite a distance ahead. "Don't you run out in the street, young man. You stay on the sidewalk until Billy and I get there."

Shea looked at Billy who was watching Ben. She noticed the likeness in his characteristics next to Ben's, they both had the same color eyes and Ben's lips were pouty, the way Billy's were. Shea had always loved Billy's lips.

She turned her attention back to Ben, feeling more content than she had in a long time.

$\mathscr{C}$HAPTER EIGHTEEN

"Christ! Whaddya mean, you don't know?" Kevin slammed his fist on the lawyer's desk.

"Just that, Kevin. This is very strange. You come waltzing in here in a tirade, claiming something about you having a son and want to see him. It's just not that easy. You're not even certain he's yours. We can't just go up to some strange woman and ask her to prove who the father of her baby is."

"She's not a stranger. I told you we had an affair. It didn't last very long, then one day out of the blue she disappeared."

"Disappeared?"

"Yeah, you know, she hit the road. Went somewhere, but didn't tell me. No note, no phone call, no nothin'."

"And she all of sudden shows up out of nowhere with this kid, and you think it's yours?"

"No, Phil, I don't think anything. I know! That kid is mine." Kevin sat back with his hands over his face. Finally he leaned forward again. "Please, Phil. I'm begging you, help me here... I'm only trying to do the right thing. A boy has the right to know his own father. I mean what kind of message are we sending, if we allow women to take their children away from their daddies?"

"You're really serious about this," Phil commented, thumping the tip of his pen on his desk blotter. "Heck, you have to admit, it is commendable. Usually it's the woman coming in here looking for the father to pay child support."

"See? You have a father who wants to be responsible if only he were given the chance. This should be easy."

"Have you tried talking to her?" Phil asked, making a note on a yellow legal pad.

"She won't see me. Look, all I want to do is see my boy. I don't care what she does. She could be married for all I know"

Kevin sat forward on his chair. "If you could have just seen the look in that boy's eyes like I did. He's my spitting image. I just want him to know he has a daddy who cares."

"Okay, Kevin. Let me research this a little bit, see what we have to do to subpoena the birth records. Do you know where the baby was born?"

Kevin shook his head. "I don't even know where she is now, but I'll pay whatever it takes to find out."

"Okay." Phil got up from his seat. "I'm going to have my assistant take down as much information as possible from you. I will probably give you a call by the end of the week. I'm not promising anything, all I can do is look into it for you."

Kevin stuck his hand out to meet Phil's. "Thank you. That's all I'm asking. Hey, thanks again, you don't know what this means to me."

Kevin got outside the door and walked off like he'd just won a duel.

◆　　　◆　　　◆

Janet Frey had turned out to be an excellent baby-sitter. She had a cheerful personality that Shea took to immediately. She was an older woman in her sixties. It was obvious she dyed her hair to cover the gray, a chore she did at home, for it looked like she'd done the work herself. Her mane was a flaming red, and she wore garish green eye shadow and bright red lipstick to top off her eccentric look. Shea had second thoughts when she'd first met her, but Ben took to her almost instantly. Shea half wondered if it wasn't the fact she looked rather clownish that Ben liked her so well. But for all her odd eccentricities she seemed genuinely warm and friendly. She told Ben to call her 'Auntie,' as that's what all the children in the apartment complex called her.

Ben had a great time his first day with her. By the time Shea had gotten home from her meetings, Ben had made enough artwork to cover even the biggest of refrigerators.

"Look what me and Auntie Janet made," he squealed excitedly.

"Oh, these are wonderful," Shea said, coming to hug him. "Did you make these for Mommy?" Ben nodded. "Well, come on honey, we'd better get going. We're meeting Billy for dinner. Would you like that?"

"Yippee! Can Auntie Janet come too?"

Shea looked surprised. "Uh...."

"No, honey," Janet broke in, "remember, Auntie Janet bowls on Monday nights."

"Oh yeah, that's right. Mommy, Auntie Janet says we're going bowling some night, too."

Shea looked at Janet in confusion.

"Oh, I almost forgot to ask you. Is it all right if Ben comes and spends the night Saturday? I'm having a slumber party."

Shea didn't quite know what to say. She'd never heard of anyone doing this before.

"Don't worry, I do this all the time. You can talk to some of the other mothers in the complex. It kind of gives the parents a night off. I take them bowling or rent a bunch of movies."

"Well, I guess that's okay. Are you sure it won't be a bother?"

"Don't be silly, these kids are my life. I love doing things like this for them. Does Ben have a sleeping bag?"

Right then Shea was glad she'd thought to bring Ben's bag with her. She'd planned to take him camping. "Yes, he does. You know, this is really great of you. I've kind of met up with an old boyfriend and we could sure use a night out together."

"Yes, I know. Ben told me about Billy."

"Really?" Shea asked astounded.

"Seems he's taken to him."

Shea smiled to herself. She still wasn't sure of what was in the future for the both of them, but Ben had never taken to Grey like he did Billy. The two got along splendidly. Of course Billy did have that childish spirit in him. Shea was delighted. It had scared her to think she'd have to take Ben away from his friends and family in Florida. But Ben loved Billy, and now he would meet some new friends this weekend at his slumber party. "What time Saturday?"

"Two would be great. I'll see you tomorrow, Ben," Janet handed him his knapsack. "I put all your art work in here, okay?"

"Uh-huh. See you tomorrow." He sprinted off down the hall.

♦   ♦   ♦

Shea was putting her earrings on when Billy knocked at the door. "Hi, you look nice." He handed her yet another bouquet of flowers.

"You're spoiling me," Shea scolded, taking them from him. "Thank you." She added them to the ones already in the vase and placed a small kiss on his cheek. Billy seemed surprised, but didn't make a big deal out of it. He knew she would have to come to him on her own terms when she was ready. He took Sam's advice. It was going to be a slow process, but if he wanted her he would have to let go and let things happen as they will. It was a hard decision, but he was determined not to screw things up this time.

"Where's Ben?" He looked around for him.

"I got rid of him for the night," she said jokingly.

"What did you do, ship him off to a work camp?"

"No actually, he's at his baby-sitter's. She wanted to keep him for the night. So.." she said, facing him. "We have the evening to ourselves."

Billy stepped back. "We're full of surprises tonight, aren't we?"

Shea gave him a warning look and Billy heeded it. "Let's go to dinner," he said, changing the subject. "I'm starved."

Shea looked out at the scenery as they went. "Where are we going for dinner?" She saw they were heading up the hill.

"There's a new barbecue place up on the hill, thought we'd go there. Is that okay?"

"Sure." Shea all of a sudden felt panicked. It was on that road that led up the hill where the rape took place. She looked out the window and realized they were getting close. She held her sweaty palms against her sides, her arms crossed tightly in front of her. Beads formed on her forehead. She remembered what the therapist had told her and she began taking deep breaths, glancing sideways to see if Billy was watching her. He seemed lost in his driving and she felt relieved he was oblivious to her distress.

She kept up the breathing until they were well past the horrible sight and heading up the mountain to Thatcher Park. She thought about all the times she and Billy had hiked through the trails up there.

Billy suddenly turned off into one of the overlooks and stopped the truck. Shea sat frozen for a moment. He got out and went around to help her down from the seat. The sun was starting to disappear behind the hills opposite. The sky was splashed with lavender streaks, making Shea think someone had taken a brush and painted them there. She walked to the stone wall and stared out into the distance. She held her arms wrapped tightly around her, shaking slightly. Billy joined her, watching closely the expressions on her face.

"It's beautiful," she finally said, trying to ease the feeling in her heart. She wasn't sure if she was still shaken from the ride up here, or if it was Billy causing these pangs.

"Remember when we use to come here?" he whispered to her. Shea nodded and wiped a tear from her cheek.

"It can be that way again," he said gently. He put his arm around her but feeling her bristle under his touch, he pulled it away again.

"Oh, Billy!" she cried. "I wish it were that easy, but it's not. We're not the same people. I'm not the same person."

Billy turned her round to face him. "That's not true, Shea," he put his hand next to her heart. "In here, in your heart you're the same. It's only your head this person has messed up. You still have the same kind, gentle spirit as you've always had."

"You don't understand, Billy." She wiped her tears again. Billy handed her his handkerchief and she blotted the area around her eyes. "The other night when you tried to kiss me...."

Billy interrupted her. "I told you that will never happen again."

"But don't you see? I wanted it to happen. It surprised me as much as it did you. I didn't want to back away from you. It just happened. Now I'm afraid I'll never be able to be loved again." She looked into his eyes. "Billy, what if I can't give you what you need?"

"Shea, you've already given me what I need. I've never been happier. Since you've come back in my life it's like I'm alive again."

"Oh, Billy. I want this to work, but I don't see how." She sniffled.

146

"Shea, I know what you're thinking about. We can work on it together. You need to learn how to trust again. Let me be the one to show you."

"I can't ask you to do that. What if I never...."

"What if we what... never have sex? Well, then we don't. I'll still be happy. Shea, you're the only one that makes me feel like this. I want to be with you, I don't care about anything else."

"I just don't know, Billy. Look, I'm not even sure I'm going to be moving back here." She dropped her hands down by her sides and gazed out into the horizon.

"We'll take it one step at a time. Trust me, it'll be okay. Come on." He took her hand. "Let's go eat."

◆　　　◆　　　◆

Shea and Billy sat back in their seats, holding their stomachs.

"I'm so full I could burst," groaned Shea.

"Me too." He studied her. "Shea?" She looked at him. "Would you come home with me tonight?"

Shea hung her head down. "I thought we weren't going to talk about that anymore?"

"We're not. I want you to come see the house. That's all, I promise... I want you to see what I've done with it."

"I'd like to see it," Shea said quietly, thinking about it.

"We can go for a walk around the lake."

"Walk off dinner," she added, giggling.

He took the check and laid some money on the table. "Come on, let's go."

It was only a few miles to the road where Billy's house was and Shea looked keenly around at the area. Not much had changed, she thought. She knew she had no reason to be scared, but she felt her palms moisten with sweat and the old familiar butterflies racing around the pit of her belly.

Billy pulled the truck into his drive and hopped out, quickly running around to help Shea. He noticed her sweater was a little light and grabbed the extra coat he always kept with him. The nights still got pretty chilly up on the hill. He wrapped the coat around her shoulders and led her down the path to the lake. The moon's glow was brightly reflecting off the water, and bonfires dotted the opposite shore. Slowly they walked down the beach.

Billy took her hand and Shea didn't resist. They walked out on one of the docks nearby and sat down next to each other. Shea got a little closer to Billy, trying to capture his warmth.

He could feel her moving closer, but remembered his promise. He basked in the warm feelings that came over him every time Shea was around. She was like a drug to him, an addiction he couldn't and didn't want to get over.

They talked about general things, Billy being careful not to bring up touchy subjects. He told her how it was living up there and about his dog Basset. They talked about Shea's job, and about the shop and the problems Billy was having there.

Shea felt herself relaxing against Billy's side. He moved slowly and smoothly until his arm was around her waist. She didn't flinch and Billy relaxed, too.

There were a couple of drops warning before they heard the loud clashing thunder, and were consumed by a raging downpour. They both jumped up and ran for the house, screeching in laughter all the way. They fell in the door, their clothes so wet they clung to their frames.

Billy ran and got a towel for Shea and helped her dry her hair. "Boy, that storm came up fast," she said, surprised.

"That's the way the weather happens up here. Don't you remember?"

Shea nodded, rubbing her hair in the towel. She peeled off Billy's jacket and placed it over the doorknob. Her blouse had remained dry except for the part in the front where the opening was.

Billy took his shoes off and ran to the bedroom for dry clothes. He handed her a pair of sweat pants and a shirt. "Here, put these on. I'll put your clothes in the dryer."

Shea stood shivering, contemplating the decision, but the coldness overtook her and she went off the bathroom as she was told.

Billy quickly changed himself and then started a fire. He poured two glasses of brandy from the decanter and waited. When Shea finally appeared in the doorway, Billy gasped at how lovely she looked. She was combing through the wet tangles of her hair. He took the comb and gently ran it through the pieces in the back.

"You look wonderful in those," he said, touching the curve of her hip.

She pulled away, but smiled. "Thank you." The words were barely audible. Shea felt her first pang of real danger. She had to call on all her strength to remain calm. Visions flashed through her mind, but they weren't bad ones. They were of another time they were up in the mountains. The firelight was playing off Billy's face then, too. They were sitting by a fire and Billy was telling her how much he loved her. They had talked about their future plans, smiling as they looked deeply into each other's eyes. Then Billy had caressed the side of her cheek.

Shea jumped. When she looked up, Billy was touching her in the same place. "Here, let me have these." He took the wet garments she held and walked into the kitchen with them. He was back at her side in a minute with a glass. "Drink this. It'll warm you up."

Shea refused to admit what she was feeling, but knew from the past that the last thing she needed was to be warmed up. She took the amber mixture from him and took a large gulp. Billy reached out to warn her but it was too late.

"You're supposed to sip that." He watched the crimson glow fall over her cheeks.

Shea breathed in deeply and stood still while the fiery liquid burned a trail all the way to the tips of her toes.

"Are you okay?" He asked, suppressing a laugh.

Shea nodded, but wasn't sure if she really was. It took a few seconds for the immediate effects to wear off, but another one quickly took its place. She felt herself getting unsteady. Billy took her arm in one hand and his drink in the other.

"Let me show you what I've done with the house."

A dog's howl interrupted them, and Billy lead Shea out to the back door to meet Basset. The large golden Labrador bounced into the porch and shook the water off, getting Billy and Shea wet in the process. Billy held on to Shea as she fell backward from the friendly jumping around. Billy quickly scolded him and pointed him in the direction of the fire. The dog went obediently and settled on the braided rug next to the fireplace.

Billy continued his tour of the house, leading Shea onto another section of the screened patio where he'd put in a Spanish style table. As Shea looked around she became aware the house was decorated almost identically to the way they used to discuss. Billy beamed, as Shea looked around the room, astonished. They went back in through the second door to the living room, Billy hesitating before showing her the master bedroom. He was careful not to go past the bedroom door.

"This is our... my room," he corrected, hoping Shea didn't notice the blunder. He hoped it would become their room. He prayed and hoped every night that Shea would come back and they'd live their lives up in the house on the hill like they had always planned. He glanced at Shea, who hadn't seemed to notice the mistake.

They went back out into the living room. Billy sat down on the couch and invited Shea to join him. She picked the corner opposite of where he was and sat carefully, folding her leg up under her.

He got up and filled her empty glass and then put the bottle on the coffee table. He sat down next to her and took her hand. She instantly put her hand up to his chest, holding him away from her. She knew the brandy was taking effect. It scared her to think about being out of control. She had emotions fighting each other inside her, a burning ache that ran through her when he touched her, and a constant fear that seemed to win out every time he was near.

Billy let go of her hand and sat back. "Shea, I told you I wouldn't do anything you didn't want me to do. I never want to hurt you or step over the bounds. I know it's been a long time, but try and remember how we used to be. I never tried anything then and I won't now. You've got to trust me."

Shea said nothing. She stared into the flames and wondered what it was she really wanted to do.

"Do you think it would be okay if I just held you?" he asked cautiously.

150

Shea stared for a long time before she slowly nodded. Billy took her hand and led her to the other end of the couch where he had been sitting. He sat back against the arm and gently pulled her down into him. She melted against his chest, fighting back tears of horror. He pulled the blanket from down from the back of the couch and opened it up over her. She snuggled down into it and after a long time, fell asleep.

Billy sat for a while, watching the dying embers. Taking one last sip of his brandy, he put the glass on the floor. He thought about how wonderful it was having Shea back in his arms, gently rubbing her hair and kissing the top of her head. He listened to her soft, steady breathing and it made him angry. He thought about this peaceful spirit that lay against him, and about the vile person that robbed her of her peace. The man who'd left her cowering like a child, her vibrancy for life gone, replaced by fear. He let himself cry for her, for what she'd been through. He wished more than anything he could make it all go away.

CHAPTER NINETEEN

Shea barely had time to unpack before Henry finalized the deal and sent her back to Albany for good. She said her tearful good-byes to Ted and Peg. She also regretfully sold her seven-year companion, her red convertible. It was time to get a family car and she'd need a four wheel drive for the snow anyway, but it still saddened her to actually hand the keys over to someone else for the last time. She knew the car would be well cared for, as Ted had bought it. Shea was glad her old friend would be staying in the family.

Ben was staying with Ted and Peg to give Shea time in Albany to get the move in order. She spent her days trying to salvage the few remaining accounts left at the company and her nights were spent looking for a place to live. Billy had helped her out. They finally located a nice townhouse in the school district Shea wanted Ben to attend.

She'd also met with Janet to set up a baby-sitting schedule. She thoroughly enjoyed her lunch with the woman; Janet seemed to know more about what Shea was feeling than she herself did, and Shea had come to think of her as a friend. She had told Janet about the rape and why she'd left New Salem. They also talked about Billy, Janet believing that true love only came around once. Shea reminisced about the old days when she and Billy were like soul-mates.

"You still are," Janet had told her. "Because soul-mates never really part. Oh, they may get lost for a few years, but they're never really apart even when they're not together."

Shea looked at her intensely. She felt this to be the situation between her and Billy as he had told her he had never forgotten her. Shea felt the same way, and now looking back on it, she knew that was why she could never get serious with Grey.

"It's not like we used to be," she sighed, pushing her salad around on her plate.

Janet put her iced tea down and took Shea's hand. "I understand what happened to you was tragic. This man destroyed your spirit, but Billy loves you. That's as plain as the sun rising every day. Don't let this criminal keep you from having the one thing you've always wanted. Give Billy a chance."

Janet was so on target that Shea squirmed in her seat. She knew in her heart what she really wanted more than anything, was to have Billy back the way they were before. Yet, her fear of intimacy kept her from returning Billy's affections.

◆　　　◆　　　◆

The day Shea had waited for had finally arrived. Ben was joining her in their new home. Ted had booked himself a flight so Ben wouldn't be traveling alone. He was going to take the opportunity get in touch with some old friends who'd moved to the area.

Shea waved out the window as they got off the plane. Seeing her, Ben ran ahead to meet her. She waited patiently inside the terminal until he made his way through the throngs of other passengers, and ran into his mother's arms. Ted sauntered in shortly after him, carrying Ben's backpack and toys. Shea laughed when she saw how frazzled he looked.

"Looks like he kept you busy," she smiled. They walked toward the baggage claim, Ben running ahead like he always did, playing with the vending machines and anything else he found along the way. Ted and Shea caught up on news as they followed Ben. When Shea mentioned Billy, Ted gave her a sideways glance of disapproval.

"I know what you're thinking, Ted. I just want you to know everything is okay, you'll see. I can't wait for you to meet him, he's waiting at home for us."

"Shea, I just don't understand how you can go back to the jerk after he hurt you so badly."

"That was all a big mistake. Billy never got married. It was just a rumor. Ted, please don't judge until you meet him."

As she expected, both Ben and Ted were famished. She was glad Billy was handling dinner, because she was hungry herself. As everything was still packed in boxes at home, dinner was just one less thing she'd have to worry about.

"The furniture arrived this morning, but nothing's been done yet," she explained. "Billy's bringing dinner. He's meeting us at the apartment, so we'd better hurry."

They got their bags and hurried to the car. Another storm had just passed through, but the sun had left a rainbow. They all gazed at it as Shea drove them to the house.

"I only have one question, Shea. If Billy was never married, then why did Sarah write you that letter?"

"I don't know. It must have been some gossip she picked up and thought I should know about."

"I suppose I should visit them while I'm here," said Ted resignedly. "I feel sort of obligated since they spent so much time and money at Mom's funeral."

"That's up to you, but I haven't seen them and don't want to. I don't even think they know I'm back. I'd like to keep it that way."

Ted nodded. "Gotcha! I won't even mention your name."

"Thanks, I'd appreciate it. I'd rather not get involved with them if I can help it."

"I guess I'm kind of looking forward to meeting this Billy. Ben's been talking about him all week."

Shea looked at Ben in the rearview mirror and smiled. "You like Billy, don't you, sweetie?"

"He's fun. He's like Ted. He plays with me. Mommy, I brought him a gun just like mine."

Shea glanced at Ted. "He kept saying he wanted another gun, so I bought him one."

"You know I hate those things."

"Well, he's going to see them everywhere anyway. All the kids in our neighborhood have them. You just have to teach him about them."

"Yeah, Mommy. You only use play guns and never point them at someone's face. Don't worry, Mom, I'm only going to shoot the bad guys, okay?" Ben rubbed his mother's hair.

Shea put her hand back and touched his hand. "You're such a little man, Ben." They pulled the car into the lot and Billy came out to meet them.

154

Ted shook his hand, then did a double-take, looking back and forth from him to Ben. If he didn't know better, he would have sworn Ben was Billy's son. The resemblance was almost scary, if you didn't know any better, you'd think he was Billy's.

Ben dashed across the parking lot toward the door.

"Ben!" called Shea. "What have you been told about running through parking lots?"

Ben sat down on the step quietly. "I'm sorry, Mom. I forgot." He waited until they got to the door before getting up. "Mom, is this our new house?"

"This is it." She put her free arm around his shoulder, guiding him up the steps that led to the dining room.

Ben immediately bolted off down the hall. "Is this my room, Mommy?" he asked, standing in the doorway.

"Yes, honey. You can play in there if you want."

Ben went into his room and looked around. He found his toy box and set about unpacking it. Shea and Billy worked all morning setting up Ben's room. Shea wanted him to feel like it was his room in Florida, carefully setting it up as it had been there.

Shea pulled the food out of its containers and then looked through some of the boxes for silverware and plates. The two men were busy moving the living room around the way she had asked. When she called them to dinner, Ted dropped his side of the sofa, scurrying off to the dining room.

"Sorry," he winked at Billy before he went. "I'm starving."

"I'm right behind you." Billy dropped his side of the sofa with a bang.

◆　　◆　　◆

After dinner Shea started to clean up. Ben had talked Billy into letting him help move the furniture around like the big guys. Shea stifled a laugh as she watched them lift the couch. Billy and Ted had either end with Ben in the middle. They sounded like a comedy act.

"Okay sport, got it. Now bring it this way. Watch your toes! Okay, set it down now." Ben got excited about helping and stayed until the whole living room was in order.

155

"Beer, anyone?" Shea held some bottles up in her hand.

"Yes!" they all piped in and laughed. Ben had called out with them, but Shea gave him a root beer. He sat down next to Billy and Ted, laughing whenever they did. Shea thought it was great the men included Ben in their conversation.

Ben actually only sat there for a few minutes before falling asleep. Shea carried him into his room and put him to bed. She pulled his jeans off but left his shirt on and covered him. Leaning over, she kissed him before leaving the room. By the time she got back to the living room, Ted was already snoring on the couch while Billy cleaned off the table from dinner.

"Hey, let's get some beers and go out on the porch," she whispered to Billy.

He gladly threw the cloth he was using back in the sink and got two beers from the fridge. They tip-toed quietly down the stairs, laughing at the noisy snores from Ted.

It was warm and balmy. The sun was just starting to disappear, but it was one of those days you knew would stay warm despite dusk. They sat down on the steps together to sip their beers.

"You look tired," said Billy, pulling Shea closer to him.

"It's been a long week." She looked toward the house. "And I still have all that unpacking to do."

"I'll help you, I'm off tomorrow anyway. What time do you want me here?"

"I can't ask you to do that, Billy. You've already done so much."

"Nonsense. I'm bringing breakfast."

Shea smiled at him and Billy leaned over to place a kiss on her lips. She pulled away at first, but then relaxed into him.

"I told you I won't don't anything unless you say it's okay."

"I'm just nervous, Billy, that's all."

"Of me kissing you?"

"No." She shook her head. "Of what comes after."

"Shea, I already told you it'll never happen, not unless you say you want to. As a matter of fact, I'm going to make you beg before I do anything." He pulled her face to his and kissed the corner of her mouth.

"It'll never happen," she murmured.

"What?"

"I'll never beg."

"You're sure 'bout that?"

"Listen to you. Has anyone ever begged before?"

"Yes," he said shyly, bowing his head. "But I had to tell her no."

Shea burst into laughter. "How do I know you won't tell me no?"

"Ah, my fair princess. Because it's you I want to marry."

Shea let out a giggle, then became very serious when she saw he wasn't laughing. "You're serious aren't you?" Her hand came up to his chest.

He nodded not looking at her. Instead he tore at the wrapper on the beer bottle. "I don't have a ring, but we can pick one out for you this weekend."

"Billy, I don't know what to say. This is so sudden."

"I know. You don't have to give me an answer right away. Think about it."

"Billy, how can you be so sure this is what you want?"

"Shea, I've never wanted anyone but you. I know in my heart that if we didn't get married I'd stay single for the rest of my life."

"Billy don't say...."

He put a finger to her lips. "It's the truth. I know that. I just hope you won't disappoint me."

Shea laid her head against his chest and he wrapped his arms around her. She didn't know how to feel. A part of her wanted this badly, but another part knew things could never be as they were.

Ted walked away from the window and smiled. He'd seen and heard everything. There was no mistaking the bond that had developed between Ben and Billy. He'd never seen that with Grey. He felt secure leaving Shea here as long as Billy was around. He knew he'd have to take a step back and let Billy be her protector. He watched Billy kiss Shea good-night, then leave. She came back up the stairs and Ted quickly went back and sat on the couch, hoping he wasn't detected.

CHAPTER TWENTY

At eight o'clock, the sun had already turned the cool morning into a sopping, scorching mess. Shea searched through the boxes in her room for something cool to wear. Pulling her hair up in a band she let a few strands fall down her back. She decided on a tank top and some shorts, then headed off to the shower. Ben was playing in his room and she asked him to let Billy in when he arrived.

She let the cool water flow over her face. She needed some coaxing this morning after Billy dropped his bomb last night. She hadn't slept a wink. Could it really be true? Would Billy ever marry again if she refused him? She wasn't even sure how she felt. All these new things coming to her all at once.

She got out and dried herself off, dressing quickly because she could hear Billy talking to Ben. She waited in the bathroom for a minute, nervous about facing him. Slowly pulling the door open, she peered out.

"Mornin', beautiful!" roared Billy.

Shea leaned back against the door, hesitant to answer. He obviously hadn't forgotten about his proposal. He'd brought breakfast over and was cutting Ben's pancakes when she finally emerged into the hall.

"Hi," he walked over to her, staring at her for a moment. "Can I kiss you?" he whispered.

"I'm exhausted," stammered Shea. "I couldn't sleep a wink after your nice little proposal last night. If you have to ask for a kiss, the answer is no." The words tumbled out of her mouth at once.

Billy grabbed her. Leaning her over, he placed a long, ardent kiss directly in the center of her mouth. Shea was taken aback and Ben laughed hysterically. She stifled a laugh and took her seat at the table.

Billy put a large cup of coffee in front of her. "Here, this ought to help."

"I should have made you beg for that kiss," sniffed Shea.

"It'll never happen. Hey, where's Ted?"

"He got up at five, took a shower, mumbled something about us needing to be alone and asked if he could borrow the car."

"Smart man."

"Is it just me, or are people trying to push us together?"

"I don't know," grinned, Billy. "Hey Ben, I asked your mother to marry me."

Shea looked up at him in shock. "Billy!"

"Cool." Ben stuffed another piece of pancake in his mouth. "Does this mean you'll be my dad? I don't have one, you know."

Billy realized what he'd done. Horrified, he looked at Shea. "I'm so sorry, Shea. I didn't know." He wanted to kick himself for not keeping quiet. "I'd better go," he mumbled, getting up to leave.

"Billy!" Shea called out. "Wait. Ben, go get washed up. Billy and I need to talk."

Ben obediently ran off to the bathroom. Billy came back into the dining room, standing at the far end of the table.

"It's not your fault, Billy. Ted told me he was asking questions while he was there." She put her coffee on the table. "I knew it would come to this eventually. He sees other kids with their dads, it's only natural he wonders."

"Have you thought about what you're going to tell him?"

"What do you tell a five year old? Your mom was raped, then she had you, and that's why you don't have a dad?" Shea put her napkin down and slumped in her chair.

Billy pulled a chair over and sat next to her. "If we got married, I could be his dad."

"Billy, I don't want to marry you just so my son can have a dad."

"So, you don't love me?"

"Yes, I do!" She said throwing her arms up in frustration. "At least I think, that is... I don't know."

"Shea, I'm inclined to believe your first comment."

"I do love you Billy, but I'm so scared."

"Scared of what?"

"I don't know. Of being intimate."

"It's the sex thing again isn't it? Damn it, Shea!" He got up and paced around the table. "Okay, then. I have a solution. We get married and never have sex. We don't talk about it or anything. I'm happy because I can spend the rest of my life with you, and you're happy because you never have to have sex. Okay?" He came over and stood directly in front of her. "We'll never talk about this again."

Shea couldn't hold back the laughter any longer. "I still say I'll never beg."

"Well, we can talk about that if the time ever comes. In the meantime, what are we going to do about Ben?"

Shea sobered. "I don't know."

"Shea, I love him like I love you. If we get married I'll adopt him."

"You make it sound so easy. He's still going to have to be told sometime."

"And we'll do that. By then he'll be old enough to understand. And we can tell him together."

"You're too much," she sputtered.

"Is that a yes?"

She nodded. She knew she couldn't deny her heart. She had done that long enough already.

"Great!" He kissed her. "I have a good lawyer, I'll call him on Monday."

Ben came running back out with his guns. "Come on, Billy. Let's play."

"Can't today, slugger. See all these boxes here? We have to unpack them. Tell you what, though, if you help your mom and me with these, I'll play with you as soon as we're done. Deal?"

Ben stuck his hand out. "Deal!"

◆   ◆   ◆

They'd worked most of the day unpacking and putting things away. Ben fell asleep at dinner, which didn't surprise either of them

160

as they had him running around helping all afternoon. They settled on the floor in the living room with a bottle of wine, to talk about their wedding plans.

"So, it'll be in the fall?" Billy repeated what Shea had just said.

"You had another time in mind?" she asked.

"Tomorrow."

"We can't do that," she grinned. "Think about it. Do you know how long our families have waited for this?"

Billy suddenly sat up. "That's right, we still have to tell my parents! This isn't going to be easy."

"Why not?" Shea wondered.

"Don't get me wrong. Mom loves you like you were her own, but when you left it hurt everyone. She took it really hard."

Shea moved from the floor to the couch. She crossed her arms in front of her as emotions swam inside her head. She hadn't realized what the full impact of her leaving had meant to everyone.

"What are we going to do?" she asked at last.

Billy joined her on the couch. "We're going to tell them. Shea don't worry about it. When you tell her what happened... we are going to tell her what happened, aren't we?"

"I hadn't thought about any of this before."

"Shea, I have to tell Mom. She's been wondering what's going on with me. I've been so happy since you've come back, it's taken everything not to tell her what I've been up to and with whom."

"What you've been up to? You've been planning this all along?" She searched his eyes.

Billy nodded bashfully. "I have been so happy since you're back in my life. I can't explain what it means to me to touch and kiss you again."

Shea couldn't stop the tears welling up in her eyes. She thought she was the only one hurt by the rape. It devastated her to know she caused so much pain to the people she loved most. "How can your mother ever forgive me, Billy?"

Billy held her close. "Shea, don't even start beating yourself up over this. Who knows what any of us might have done if we were in your situation? Mom has never stopped loving you."

Shea realized since Aunt Vicki had died, she really didn't have anyone to turn to. She had been lonely for that female bond she no longer had. Billy's mother, Naomi, had been there as much as Billy had when her parents died, but she still felt a twinge of fright at the thought of opening up to her. She knew Naomi well enough to know what can happen if you hurt one of her children. Still, she needed to mend the fences between them.

They set up a time for the next day to go visit. Shea was beginning to feel sleepy, but the conversation had also made her realize how much she missed Vicki. "Billy, I don't want to be alone. Will you stay with me tonight?"

He kissed her temple lightly and then helped her up off the couch. "Come on, let's go to bed."

Shea went in the bathroom and changed into the extra long football shirt she used as a nightdress. Billy stripped down to his underwear, taking off his shirt but leaving his T-shirt on underneath. He was sitting up in bed when she came out. "I hope you don't mind. I can't sleep in jeans."

"No," she said nervously, standing next to the bed.

Billy pulled the covers back. He reached over and took her hand, gliding her gently onto the bed next to him. She slid down under the covers, keeping a space between them.

"You're shaking," he observed curtly.

"I'm okay," she said in a small voice.

"Shea, I'm not going to hurt you. I made a promise, and besides, you've been drinking. When and if we finally make love I want you to be totally aware of what's going on. I don't have to stay if you feel threatened."

Shea laid back against the pillow, her body relaxing into the sheets. "No, I'm fine. Please, Billy just bear with me."

Billy pulled the covers up over them and moved closer to her. He caressed her arm until she melted into him, slowly losing consciousness. Billy couldn't go to sleep right away, so he lay awake, running his fingers through the silvery strands of her hair. He breathed in the aroma of her perfume, reminiscing about the times he held her while they slept by the fire on their camping trips. He couldn't believe she was actually lying here next to him again.

◆   ◆   ◆

Billy came up behind his mom and hugged her so tight, her feet came off the ground. She turned and swatted him with the towel she had been holding.

"To what do I owe this great treat? I haven't seen you in weeks."

"I know," apologized, Billy. "I've been busy... dating."

His mother looked at him in shock. She threw her big strapping arms around him and gave him a bear hug. It almost knocked the breath out of him and it took a few seconds before he was able to catch his breath.

"So, tell me about this wonderful person who sure has put the life back into you."

"Oh, Mom. She's beautiful and caring and loving... and I brought her over to meet you."

Naomi screeched. "Not now, son!" She pulled her hair up into a pony tail behind her. "I look a mess."

"Don't worry," Billy laughed. "I know she's going to love you." He went to the door and opened it.

Naomi couldn't see past the screen door. When Billy opened it she stared in shock as Shea walked into the kitchen. She immediately looked down to hide the hurt on her face.

Billy pushed Shea toward her and went to the refrigerator for something to drink. He got out iced tea and four glasses. Ben stood behind Shea, hiding his face from the strange lady standing before him. Billy poured the tea and then took Ben by the hand.

"You two have some talking to do. We'll be in the basement."

He made a hasty exit, taking Ben with him. Shea turned quickly to catch him, but he was gone. She stood nervously, not knowing what to say. She now realized what her leaving had done to everyone.

"Can we sit down and talk?" Shea asked, barely able to say the words.

Naomi shrugged and sat in a chair. She dried her hands on the apron she was wearing, keeping her head bowed.

"I know you must hate me," Shea started to say.

"I don't hate you," answered Naomi. "I love you. But you hurt me, hurt Billy."

Shea sat down in the chair next to Naomi. "I know that now. I never meant to hurt anyone. I love all of you, Billy most of all." She reached for a glass and poured some tea into it, taking a large gulp before continuing. "I left because I felt there was nothing else for me to do. You see something bad happened, and I got scared...."

"Is that where the boy came from?" asked Naomi. Shea nodded, grateful that Naomi understood what happened. "I'm sorry," was all she said.

Shea didn't elaborate on the subject anymore and Naomi didn't push her.

"Naomi, Billy and I decided we needed to come and talk to you and Dad, if he'll still let me call him that."

"He still considers you his daughter. He loves you."

"Well then, Billy and I have some news we would like to share with both of you." She took another sip of tea and looked at Naomi. She seemed a little warmer now toward her. "Billy and I are getting married."

Naomi looked up at Shea. Wiping a tear away with the towel she hugged her. Naomi held her tight, not wanting to let go for fear she'd lose her again. Then she spoke, saying all the things she would have said if Shea had even gotten in touch with her. They stayed in each other's arms, trying to recapture all the things they had lost. Naomi her future daughter-in-law, and Shea the mom she depended on after her own had died. Shea realized how much that family had meant to her and how much she had lost. She was sure now she was making the right decision by marrying Billy. He was the only one she'd ever really loved and it was good to know his family still loved her too.

Billy came into the room with Ben in tow. "Have you two talked?" he asked cautiously.

They both nodded and then broke out in a jubilant laugh. Ben, being protective of his mother, ran to her and put his arm around her.

"Are you sad, Mommy?" His little voice melted her heart as usual.

Shea shook her head. "No, Mommy is very happy, honey. Say hello to your new grandma." She turned him to face Naomi. Ben looked at her for a few moments, not knowing what to do. Naomi held her arms out to him and he carefully went to her. "This is Billy's mom, Ben. Since Billy and I are getting married, she'll be your grandma. Do you understand?"

Ben nodded, but wondered about the husky woman holding him on her lap.

"I'll bet Ben would like some cookies," said Naomi.

Ben got an excited look on his face as Billy went to the cookie jar and took out a handful of fresh baked chocolate chips. He gave Ben two, offering one to Shea. She declined so he popped the rest of the clump in his mouth.

They talked for a while before Naomi suggested they go upstairs and tell her husband, Jake, about their plans. He still didn't know who was sitting downstairs. He'd been confined to bed for the past few months, getting up very rarely, and then only when his nurse was there to supervise him.

He'd heard the voices, but never imagined it would be Shea. He never stopped loving her and hadn't harbored any ill feelings toward her when she left. He knew in his heart there must have been a good explanation for her taking off like she did. He also knew when the time was right she'd be back. He saw the way Shea and Billy acted around each other. They were destined to be together.

Naomi burst through the door with Shea on her arm. "Look who's back!" she exclaimed excitedly.

It took a few moments for Jake to see who it was. Shea walked up to the side of the bed and placed a kiss on his cheek. He grabbed her and pulled her close to him, making her lose her balance. He didn't let her go for a while. When she looked at him she could see there were tears starting to form at the corners of his eyes. She held him for a minute before backing away.

"It's good to see you, Dad."

165

"I've missed you," he said in a whisper.

Several strokes had left Jake fragile. He'd lost the use of some of his faculties and needed almost constant care now. But his mind was still spry and you still couldn't get much past him. He still understood all Billy told him about the shop, giving him advice when he felt it was needed.

Shea told him about the wedding and introduced him to Ben. He never asked any questions about the boy and Shea was thankful for that. Telling another woman about rape is much easier than trying to explain it to a man. She knew Naomi would tell him about it later, so it got her off the hook.

Jake accepted Ben happily. He was thrilled she and Billy were finally getting married. He'd waited many years for this moment.

Naomi and Shea talked some more in the kitchen while Billy and Ben stayed with Grandpa. Naomi wanted a big splendid affair. She felt she had waited long enough for it to take place. It was important to have the wedding as soon as possible because of Jake's condition. He would definitely be attending if they had to bring him in his bed. He would never miss the event they'd all waited so long for!

CHAPTER TWENTY-ONE

It had been three weeks since Billy and Shea announced their engagement to Billy's parents. Naomi wasted no time getting the preparations started, running Shea ragged all over town. First there was a dress, then there were invitations, the cake, flowers and oh, so much more to do. Shea got exhausted just thinking about it all.

If Billy and Shea had wanted a small wedding, it was nothing they had control over anyway. Naomi stepped right in taking over the entire event. Billy and Shea both decided to let her have the wedding she wanted. After all, she and Jake had waited almost twenty-six years for this. It made Shea feel like part of the big happy family she'd belonged to once before. Billy had been so great, taking Ben every night. He'd taken him bowling, fishing, and even horseback riding. Shea was delighted that Grandpa Jake got in on the action, playing video games with Ben in the den. All Shea's fears were calmed now. Ben had fit into the family like he had always been a part of it. Even Grey, whom Ben loved, had never been able to penetrate the shield the little boy had always kept up. He'd always been so protective of his mom, but with Billy it was different. He was relaxed and confident around him. She hated to admit it, but Ben had grown into the relationship better than she.

She stood chopping celery and listening to her two men playing in the bathroom. Bath time was always a myriad of exciting adventures. They were always blowing up something or shooting it out with the bad guys. She listened to them now as they torpedoed some foreign enemy territory. With each bomb came a splash of water. Shea knew by now the floor was probably soaked. Pulling the bread out of the oven she carefully placed it on the stove top, then sneaked off to the bathroom to watch the two loves of her life. She enjoyed watching them play together, it reminded her of the

167

days when she was little, when she and her mom would play hair-dresser in the tub.

"Dinner's almost ready," she announced, taking a towel from the bar.

Billy turned and shot her a grateful glance. "You're soaked, Billy. Why don't you go get changed and I'll get him ready for bed?"

It was common for Ben to eat earlier than she and Billy. He always got hungry early and his bedtime was seven o'clock. This gave Shea and Billy a chance to eat in peace and catch up on the events of the day, which lately had been plenty.

Shea still stayed at her own place during the week, but they had been spending the weekends up at the cabin. Ben loved to fish and horseback ride.

Billy got up from where he was, flinging his shirt off over his head. He passed through the narrow space between the sink and Shea, pressing up against her as he left. Shea's heart quickened and she leaned back against the wall, grasping the towel rack for support. She felt the heat from his body as he crossed in front of her. Maybe it was the steam from the bathtub that made her feel so weak, but she knew better. Billy had played her just right, locking her eyes with his as he swept by. He had not taken his eyes off her until he was around the corner. Shea didn't move until he was clean out of sight.

She wobbled to the tub and got Ben out, rubbing him down briskly as if trying to put the image of the past minute out of her mind.

"Ow, Mommy. You're rubbing too hard."

"Sorry, Ben." He brushed his teeth while Shea let the water out of the tub and straightened up. When she finished putting his pajamas on, she led him to his room, being careful to look and see where Billy was. He was still in his room, changing. Shea moved quicker so he wouldn't see her.

Basset bounded into Ben's room and plopped on the floor next to the bed. Ben kissed his mom goodnight, patting Basset, too. Then he looked up at her. "Mommy, I want to say goodnight to Daddy, too."

Billy came in the room just then, and Shea left without looking at him. She practically ran to the kitchen and began ripping lettuce for the salad. She heard Billy tell Ben a short bedtime story, then all too soon he was leaning against the counter next to her. Shea could feel his eyes on her, and tried to ignore them, focusing on what she was doing. Flushing, she knew Billy was aware of the reaction he caused. She couldn't look at him, wouldn't.

Billy smiled to himself, knowing how his gaze affected Shea. "Maybe I should finish that," he said, taking the beaten up lettuce leaf from her. Again he brushed close to her, feeling the static.

"What did you think you were doing in there?" she demanded angrily.

He looked at her, surprised. "My shirt was wet. I have to take off one shirt before I can put on another." He was erupting with pleasure, at the thought of the torment he knew he was responsible for. "You've never seen a man with his shirt off before?"

Shea turned away from him. He could be so maddening sometimes, but he was right. Why should the sight of him without a shirt bother her? She'd seen plenty of men without their shirts on.

"Did I offend you?" He brushed his lips against her ear.

Shea felt a burst of electricity rip through her. His breath on her neck sent chills all through her body. Billy stayed there a moment before breaking away to pour them both a glass of wine. He knew what Shea was feeling. He'd sensed the vibrations from her the last few times they were together.

Shea picked at her fingernails, unable to look at him. She knew what he was getting at and she couldn't deny him much longer. Or herself.

"Is there something wrong?" He moved close to her.

Shea stood frozen, unable to will herself to move. She shook her head.

"Are you afraid?" he gently pried.

She looked up at him. "I don't know."

He handed her the glass and took her by the hand. "Come. Let's go sit by the fire. We can talk about it." He lifted the hand he was holding and kissed it.

169

Shea paused for a moment before putting the wine down on the table. "Billy, I think I'd like to stay sober tonight." She smiled at him and he knew.

He put his wine down and shut off the kitchen light. He gently lifted her up and carried her to the bedroom. Carefully, he put her down and the large feather comforter swallowed her up. She felt his strong body closing over hers and she let out a whimper.

"Don't be afraid," he whispered, letting his warm breath fall over her earlobe. He kissed it gently, creating a burning path across her cheek to her lips. He searched the depths of her mouth with his tongue. She reached out to his until they met in a swirling cascade, devouring each other like a whirlpool. He tasted every last inch of her mouth before tracing a searing path down her neck. He removed the cut-off sweatshirt she was wearing to continue his caresses.

Shea moved her hands across Billy's back, digging at his flesh in excitement. She let another groan escape. Billy continued kissing her, tasting her skin. He pulled the strap of her bra down, exposing her breast. Touching the nipple with his fingers, he took it in his mouth, suckling her soft flesh into hard rosy peaks. First one then the other, making her whimper in pleasure. Gently, he left a trail of hot, fiery kisses down along her abdomen to the luscious triangle between her legs.

The hot, tingling sensation Shea experienced had turned into a full fledged fury. All her fears drifted away from her. The ache in the pit of her stomach reached down to the depths of her loins. She tried to pull back from Billy, but he held her still. She was going to go mad with passion. Slowly, as if they had a will of their own, her hips arched to meet the catalyst of her pleasure.

"Billy I want you inside me," she groaned.

"Not yet," he whispered. "Let me love you." Carefully he moved his tongue in and out of her tunnel, playfully flicking the place between her lips.

She cried out, but he paid no attention. She covered her face with a pillow to keep from yelling out loud. "Please, Billy," she silently pleaded.

He made a path back up her stomach taking her breast again, maneuvering himself so his penis was at her opening. Her hips arched and flipped beneath him.

He covered her mouth with his as he gently entered her, moving with a gradual motion, slowly leading a path deep inside her. Then moving back and forth, he picked up the pace, sliding deeper and deeper.

Shea worked faster, and Billy followed her cues, giving her what she needed and wanted. She didn't hold back, gladly taking what she'd needed for all these years.

He pulled her hips up to meet him, gyrating furiously until he released his love inside her. Shea let out a cry of satisfaction, pulling Billy down on top of her.

They lay still for a moment, basking in the after-love, holding each other as if to never let go.

"Shea!" Billy pushed himself back up so he could see her. "Did I hurt you?" he asked, rubbing her cheek.

Shea shook her head. "No," she whispered, reaching out to take his arm. "I was so afraid right up until it happened. I never... never knew it could be like this."

"This is the way it's supposed to be, my love. This is what it's all about." He pulled her close, encircling her in his arms. "What happened to you was not love. It wasn't even sex. It was violence."

Shea lay back with a sleepy smile and stared at her beloved. "Thank you for being patient with me and for showing me how wonderful making love is."

Billy pulled her even closer, planting a stream of small kisses over her eyelids. He watched as Shea's lids grew heavy and her breathing became a soft, even motion. He took in her beauty, watching every inch of her breast rise and fall with her breathing. For a long time watched her gentle features before slipping off to sleep himself.

◆　　　◆　　　◆

Shea awoke with a start, turning to watch Billy sleeping beside her. His serene features gleamed in the soft moonlight.

171

He looks so helpless, she thought with a mischievous flicker of wonderment. With playful wickedness, she lifted the covers, peeking at the vital piece she would soon possess. Two can play this game, she said, thinking about her insistent begging she'd promised she'd never do. Slowly and calculating, she moved her tongue back and forth across the tip of his vitality, manipulating it ever so gently into a sturdy stiffness.

Billy shuddered, but didn't open his eyes. He let out slow, groaning cries, rousing to the soft, moist oracle surrounding him. On the verge of delirium, he sat up fast.

"Shea, what are you doing?"

Shea pushed him back down. "Let me love you," she proclaimed, taking charge.

Billy fell back with a lustful groan. "Shea, what are you doing to me?" He squirmed under her inflaming persuasion. His excitement built as Shea worked, strategically increasing her merciless teasing.

Billy moved more fervently, pleading with her to take him. "Shea, I'm going to come, please."

"Billy, are you begging me, my sweet?" Her tone was mischievous.

"Oh, God," he moaned, pulling her on top of him.

Shea obligingly straddled him, teasing him mercilessly with her web of love. "Is this what you want?" she asked, rubbing her soft mound over his hard mass. Shea reached beneath her and took his manhood in her hands circling the tip of it just outside her pool. Billy thrust himself inside her, breaking her hands away and forcing his throbbing penis deep into her.

Shea let out a triumphant laugh, pushing herself down hard over him. They worked together in a reckless effort. Reaching higher and higher to their peak until Billy could hold back no longer, he let his bounty flow into her, like a river flowing fiercely over the edge of the fall.

Shea fell back in a trembling passion, blissfully dreaming of the moment. Billy took her hands and pulled her down over him, her soft curls cascading over his chest. His eyes drove a jubilated look of conquest through her soul.

"I never expected it to be like this either, my love," he said in contented adoration. "You have given me more than I could ever desire. I thought I was in love, but this, this feeling goes beyond what I could ever define. I can't describe how I feel, but I don't want it to ever end. I want you with me always."

Shea smiled down at him, blissfully happy herself. "You've taught me something I never thought I could have. You have given me so much, how could I have ever mistrusted you?"

"Shh," he put his finger to her lips. "It's over, now. We're together forever."

She could feel him getting hard inside her again. He rolled her over on her back and took from her the one thing she'd promised him forever. They sealed their devotion together, uniting as one.

When Shea woke up again, the sun was already casting heat through the bedroom window. She turned over to find the space next to her empty. Quickly getting up she tied Billy's robe around her. Ben's bed was empty too. She trudged over to the coffee maker and found a note. 'Gone fishing! Love, your boys.' She smiled and got a cup to put her coffee in. After adding cream, she plodded off down the trail leading to the lake. She could hear the boys talking. Walking up onto the dock she watched her two men sitting at the end, with fishing poles hanging off the edge.

Billy turned and saw her. He put his pole down and went to her side. "Good morning, gorgeous. Did you sleep well?"

"I had erotic dreams all night, I don't know what caused them," she whispered seductively. "Tell me, Mr. Kendall do you always make passionate love to someone and then go fishing?"

"Well, I don't smoke," he answered back, kissing her.

"Oh, I wouldn't say that," she teased. She walked back down to the end of the dock with him.

"Mommy, I'm fishing," Ben piped up.

"I see that." She bent down to untangle his line. "I'll make breakfast. Anyone hungry?"

"Yeah, Mommy. I want pancakes."

"Ben, you already had breakfast," admonished Billy.

"I know, Daddy, but I want pancakes now."

Billy shook his head in bewilderment.

"Get used to it. He's my teeny, weenie compact machine. He can single-handedly eat anyone brave enough to dare him out of house and home."

Billy snickered. "I'd swear he was a Kendall. I used to eat like that."

"I remember." She went back to the house to start breakfast, turning one last time to smile at Ben and Billy talking, their heads close together.

♦   ♦   ♦

Shea tucked Ben into his bed and closed the door behind her. "That's very strange. He's never asked to take a nap before. He must be really tired. What time did you get him up?"

Billy looked up from the paper he was reading. "It was quarter to five when he woke me up," he sneered, playfully.

Shea looked at him with pity. "Sorry. Could you keep an ear out for him while I take a shower?"

"Sure," he didn't look up from his reading.

Shea got into the shower and let the cool water run over her face. It felt good, breaking the heat that was already shaping up for the day. She rubbed shampoo into her hair and worked it into a foamy lather. Throwing her head back, she let the water course over her, lounging in its luxury. It wasn't often she could take a shower in peace, not with a five year old anyway.

She jumped against the sudden tongue upon her breast. "Billy, what are you doing in here?" she asked in a panicked tone. "Where's Ben?"

"He's out like a light," he answered, moving up to cover her mouth with his. His hand took hold of the back of her head pushing his lips hard into hers. He tasted every inch of her mouth.

Her knees weakened as his fingers searched the slit between her legs. Lightly he caressed the band of excitement buried in her mound. A moan escaped her. She fell to her knees taking his hardening mass in her lips.

Billy let her suck him a moment before joining her on the floor of the tub. Kneeling, he brought her down on top of him, sliding his throbbing rod deep inside her, the water beating down on them in rhythmic motion. He found her mouth again and devoured her, tasting her, basking in its fiery passion.

Shea surrendered herself in pleasurable madness. They took from each other savagely, fulfilling their needs, greedily seizing what they wanted, ignoring all else around them. They hastened their fury to take until they succumbed to their exhausted exhilaration.

They held each other, Billy teasing her nipple with the tip of his tongue. Shea put her head back under the running shower and let it fall over her.

"Oh, Mrs. Kendall look what you do to me."

"Ms. Parks," she corrected, kissing him again.

"Six weeks." He flicked her nipple playfully. "I don't know if I can wait that long."

"We don't have a choice."

"We always have a choice." He left a trail of kisses up her neck.

"Billy, now hush. Your mom would die if we got married without her knowing. Besides she's got it all planned."

"Damn my mother."

"She's worked hard to make our day special. The least we can do is wait until then."

"The waiting is the hardest part. I want you here with me all the time, forever."

"It will be that way, my love. You just have to be patient."

"Patience! I've waited twenty-six years for this. I'd say that was patient, wouldn't you?" He took her mouth again.

"Seems like a lifetime." She accepted his mouth over hers, the words lost in another passionate frenzy.

CHAPTER TWENTY TWO

Shea gave herself one last look in the mirror. The sequins on her midnight-blue satin dress sparkled in the soft glowing lights of the limo. Her hair had been swept up into a chignon, held in place by a comb of dazzling stones. She fidgeted in the seat next to Billy, knowing full well his eyes were fixed on her. He still evoked a reaction in her even if it was involuntary. It concerned her that he was in full control of her emotions at this point.

"What's on your mind?" she asked, not looking at him.

He moved closer, careful not to muss her dress. "I'm thinking about after the engagement party when we're home all alone," he whispered softly in her ear. "I'm going to take those pins from your hair one by one, nibbling on your ear while I do it and throw them on the floor. Then I'm going to take you in my arms and devour you inch by scrumptious inch, until you become putty in my hands. And then, my sweet, I'm going to eat you slowly and methodically, tasting every last morsel of your being." He traced a finger over the smooth fabric of her dress. "Are you wet?"

"You're making me crazy," she breathed.

"Just giving you something to think about," he teased with a breath upon her ear.

"You're devious, Billy Kendall!"

The limo pulled up in front of the restaurant. Shea moved to get out, but Billy caught her. "Until later," he kissed her cheek.

Shea licked her lips with a smile before getting out of the car. When she walked in and saw everyone, she felt almost sad Ben couldn't be there to meet his new family. He'd had a fever the past few days, Shea thought it best he stay home. She felt equally bad Janet had stayed home with him, but Janet insisted he stay with her. After all, he knew her and she couldn't imagine the boy staying with a stranger when he needed the comfort of someone he loved.

Shea looked in disbelief at the packed room. "I didn't know you had so much family," she commented to Billy.

"Your family is here, too." He pointed out Ted and Peg.

Shea was surprised to see Sarah sitting with them. "My cousin came to our engagement party?" she asked in disgust.

"Mom thought she had to at least ask them. I told her how you felt about it, but she insisted. They're family," he grunted.

"Who's that with her?"

"My brother," Billy said, waving at some friends of his. "We don't have to talk to them. Mom already said we could ignore them. She just felt she had to invite your Aunt Caroline and her family."

"It's okay, I can just ignore them. I have this long."

Billy led Shea to their table and pulled her chair out. "After dinner we'll have to do the mingling thing so you can meet all these people. I haven't seen half of them in years myself. You probably know most of them."

Shea let out a small laugh. "There's your sister," she said excitedly. I can't wait to say hello to her." She pointed out Billy's half-sister, Brenda, whom she'd talked to a lot when she came to visit.

Shea glanced again at the stranger sitting with Sarah. He gave her an eerie feeling, staring back at her from under his black hat. The only picture Shea had seen of Billy's brother was when he was ten. This sullen man bore no resemblance to that smiling boy. Shea pulled her shawl closer over her shoulders. Looking away, she turned her attention to the salad the waitress had set in front of her. There was something that just wasn't right about him.

Shea picked at her dinner. She deliberately kept up an animated conversation with the people at her table, avoiding looking at Sarah's companion, who bored through her with his eyes.

"Excuse me Billy, I'm going to go call and see how Ben is doing."

Billy rose to pull Shea's chair out for her. "Give him my love too, darling."

"I will." She smiled again at the thought of Billy becoming

Ben's father. The adoption papers were in the works. As soon as they were married, Ben would be able to take Billy's name. *Benjamin Kendall*, the words ran through her head. Plucking a quarter out of her purse, she dialed Janet's number. "Hi, how is he?"

"He's fine. Fast asleep, and kept his dinner down."

Shea could hear the smile in Janet's voice. "Oh, that's good. If he was the same way tomorrow, I was going to take him to the doctor. Will you tell him Mommy and Daddy love him? Thanks. Love you! Bye." Hanging up the phone she turned to go into the ladies room. She was stopped by the stranger in the hat.

"Fancy meeting you here," came a well-remembered voice.

As it registered, Shea froze, ice running through her veins. She gaped up into those eyes in disbelief. She realized now. The man sitting with Sarah, it was *him*. The monster who'd attacked her that night she accepted the ride, that horrible ride she could never forget. She took a step back.

"What are you doing here?" She kept her tone ice cold.

"I was invited," he answered smugly. "See, you don't know this, but Billy is my brother."

Shea's jaw, dropped. "Liar."

"I'll bet you wish I were, but I'm not. I'm the brother no one ever talked about. I came to wish him the best. See, you're both gonna need it. I know that's my boy you have. I'm gonna be his daddy."

Shea glared at him in rigid contempt. *"Billy's* his dad."

"Can you prove it? You're going to have to." Kevin moved close to Shea, staring down at her in triumph. "Billy isn't his dad. I am and a blood test will prove it. The boy has a right to see his father, you know. Just ask any court in New York."

"You raped me! There's not a court in this land that will let you see him after what you did."

"That's where you're wrong, see... 'cos there's no police report and you can't prove you were raped. I say it was a love affair gone wrong. You can't punish me for trying to be a good father. There's not a judge alive who'll say any different. They'll stand behind me all the way. After all, I'm a father who's been kept from seeing his boy, who wants to take care of him and be a proper dad to him. He deserves it. Every boy needs his dad." He leaned toward Shea. "Of course, it would be better if his mom and dad lived together."

Shea pushed past him. "You bastard! You'll see him over my dead body. Ben is not your son and never will be." Running from the restaurant, she hurried to the limo. "Take me to the Colonie Towers." She slipped the driver a fifty. "After you drop me off, you're done."

"But ma'am, I was hired by...."

"I don't care who hired you. I'm telling you when you drop me off you're done for the evening. Now hurry."

"Yes ma'am." He sped off down the road.

Kevin returned to the reception hall and talked with a couple people he knew. Billy kept a watch on the door, wondering what was keeping Shea.

"I expect she's in the ladies room," his mother said to his questioning look.

Billy nodded. "You're probably right. I was just wondering if Ben was all right."

His mom patted his hand. People were coming up to congratulate him. After making excuses for Shea's absence for a few minutes, he went to look for her.

◆　　　◆　　　◆

At the Colonie Towers, Shea pounded on the security buzzer until Janet answered. "Let me in!"

"Shea?"

"Yes, please let me in."

Janet pushed the entrance button, then went to the door to meet her. She was afraid, hearing a definite strain in Shea's voice. Shea tore out of the elevator, almost running her down. They went back into the apartment together, Shea hardly coherent.

"What on earth...?" demanded Janet.

"Something terrible has happened!"

"Is Billy all right?"

Shea stopped, mid thought. Billy, what was she going to tell him? He couldn't know. Even he couldn't help her now. "Yes,"

179

she stammered. "Billy's fine, but I've got to get out of here. Where's Ben?"

Janet grabbed Shea by the arm. "Get a hold of yourself. Tell me what's going on."

"It was *him*. He showed up at the engagement party...." Her words were barely audible. She pushed past Janet, dashing down the hall.

"Shea, please. He's sleeping."

"Janet, don't stop me! That man, the one who raped me... he's back. He's Billy's half-brother... how could I not have known? I should have recognized him, even if I hadn't seen him since he was a kid!" In rage she slammed her fist against the wall. "He's after Ben. I have to get out of here or he's going to take my son from me."

Janet tackled Shea in the hall with all her might. "Shea, stop! I understand, but you can't run. What about Billy, your plans?"

"Billy," repeated Shea slowly getting up again. "He can't help me, no one can. I gotta leave... take my son out of here." She paced up and down the hall in a frenzy. "I can't let him get Ben. How could I have been so stupid? I should have known it would never work." Her breath came in short gasps. "How come I didn't know who he was? I've known Billy all my life, I should have known about him."

Janet held her firmly. "Shea, you can't just leave. Let Billy help you. He loves you and Ben so much, trust in him."

"I can't believe this is happening!" howled Shea, finally breaking down into tears.

Janet led Shea to the kitchen and put some water on to boil. Going to Ben's room, she returned with a knapsack. "Here, why don't you change? You left these in Ben's bag." She handed Shea a pair of cut-off shorts and the sweatshirt.

Taking them, Shea looked in on her sleeping son. She bent down and kissed him, wiping away the tear she'd spilled on his face. She would do whatever it took to keep her child from the clutches of that monster. Ben was all that mattered. Nothing or no one would ever take him away from her. She changed her clothes and joined Janet back in the living room.

180

"Here." Janet put a cup down in front of Shea. "It's tea."

Sipping at the brown liquid, Shea thought about her next move. She was convinced she couldn't stay here and let that monster take her child away. Nothing of her despair showed on her face as she sorted through her options.

"Feeling better?" Janet asked, leaning back in her recliner.

Shea looked up momentarily. "Ah... yes. Thank you." The buzzer sounded again, making Shea jump. "Don't answer it," she pleaded. "I know it's Billy. Please don't tell him I'm here."

"I don't like lying, Shea."

"Please, I'm begging you. I'll talk to him tomorrow, but please tell him I'm not here. I'll never ask you to do anything like this again, but please."

Janet shook her head and pushed the button to speak. "Who is it?"

"Billy. Is Shea there?"

Janet looked at Shea. "Ah, no Billy, she went home."

"Is Ben okay?"

"Yes, sleeping like a log."

"Thanks, Janet. Sorry to bother you. Good night." Billy let go of the button and went back to his truck. He couldn't imagine what would make Shea leave on such short notice if it wasn't Ben. He put the truck in drive and headed off to Shea's house.

"I didn't like doing that," scolded Janet. "I still think you ought to talk to him."

"I can't, right now. Don't you see? No one can help me with this, not even Billy. Especially not Billy." Shea wondered how things could have gotten so out of hand. Could Billy have known about it? She'd told him the man said his name was Kevin. He must have talked to his brother, but then she remembered Billy hated Kevin and barely spoke to him. He'd even told her he suspected it was Kevin stealing the money from the company. He probably didn't know, but it didn't matter. He couldn't help her anyway.

No one could protect her and Ben from the courts. She knew there were no police reports from that night. Even the hospital report had disappeared. There was nothing to back her up. It was her word against Kevin's. The possibility was too risky. She'd have to leave. Go some place where she and Ben would never be found. Hawaii! That was it. Grey had invited her numerous times. No one would think to look for them there."

Janet broke into her silence. "What are you going to do?"

Shea bit at her bottom lip. "I don't know yet," she lied.

"Why don't you stay here tonight? You can sleep with Ben."

"Thanks, I will. I don't know what I'd do without you." Shea hugged Janet and went into Ben's room. Crawling in next to him, she lay for a while, breathing in the clean smell from his bath. His soft, blonde curls were pressed against the pillow. She would miss Janet, considering her a very close friend. Ben loved her, too. How she wished there were some other way. But there just wasn't. She knew she'd be hurting everyone again, but some day she hoped she'd be able to explain everything. Ben's well-being came first. He was the only one that mattered.

Getting up she went to the window to look out over the court-yard where streetlights flooded the ground. She remembered when Ben was a baby, and how he nestled up to her to sleep. She thought about Billy, her sweet wonderful Billy. She knew this would rip him apart. She vowed she'd get hold of him somehow whenever she reached where she was going. Maybe they could be together somewhere else, but it would never be New Salem, she knew that now.

How could things have gotten this messed up? Shea didn't sleep the rest of the night. She got up before the sun rose and went into the living room. She tried to flick through the channels on television, but shut it off again, only finding news. She wandered around the apartment for the next hour until Ben woke up. She ran to greet him, pulling him close to her.

"How's my boy?" she asked.

"Good, Mommy. What are you doing here, did you stay over-night, too?"

"Yes, honey, I did. I slept right here next to you."

"How come you weren't there when I woke up?" he asked through sleepy eyes.

"Because I got up earlier than you. I was out in the living room." She looked at his innocent face and almost cried. He was so excited when he found out Billy would be his dad. This would break his heart, but someday she would explain it all to him.

Janet tapped on the half open door and let herself in. "We're all up early," she smiled.

"Yes, we wake up early at our house."

They all went into the kitchen where Janet put on the kettle. Shea looked through the cupboards for the cereal, then got Ben a bowl.

"I have to go do something this morning," Shea announced. "Can I leave Ben with you for a while?"

"I'm not sure I like the sound of that."

"I'll only be a while, then I promise I'll be back. I need to talk to Billy, that's all." She hoped Janet couldn't tell she was lying.

"You know Ben is always welcome to stay here."

"I need some shoes. All I have are my heels."

Janet got a pair of tennis shoes she'd only used twice. "Here, try these. I've hardly worn them."

Shea sat on the chair and tried one shoe on her foot. "Perfect."

"I'm glad someone can use them," replied Janet. "You're going to need the car, too?"

Shea didn't meet her eyes. "Could I?"

Janet nodded with a smile. "The keys are on my dresser."

Shea quickly got the keys and headed out the door.

"Mommy, I wanna go."

"Sweetie, you stay here. Mommy won't be long." She went back to give her son a kiss, and then was gone.

◆   ◆   ◆

Billy looked at his watch then back at the house. It was eight o'clock. Time had passed by slowly. He'd camped out in his truck waiting for Shea to return home. He'd dozed for a while, but it didn't look like he'd missed anything. He got out of his truck and went up to Shea's door again. He rang the bell and waited. As he looked around, he noticed the screen door was ajar. It hadn't been the night before. Opening it he banged on the inside door loudly.

"Shea, open up. We need to talk."

There was still no answer. Billy let the screen door slam again and turned to go. It was then he noticed the envelope on the step. He picked it up. The return address was from the attorney's office. He knew it was about the adoption which he was a part of, so he opened it. As he skimmed through it his heart froze.

"Oh, my God!" He hissed, running to the truck. Now everything made sense. He knew what she'd been running from. It was his brother, Kevin. He was at the party last night. That's when she disappeared. Throwing the truck in drive, Billy peeled out of the parking lot as fast as he could.

"Damn him, the bastard." He felt such rage that he knew he'd kill Kevin when he saw him. He sped toward the Towers again, not bothering to stop for the lights.

When he got to Janet's apartment, he jumped out of the truck and ran to the door. He pounded the bell until she answered.

"Janet, it's Billy. Let me up, I know Shea's there. Look, I understand everything, now. I need to talk to her."

Janet buzzed him in and waited at the door. When he burst in, Ben squealed in delight.

"Hi, Daddy!"

Billy went to him and picked him up long enough to hug him. "Hi, pal. How are you?" He mussed his hair before turning back to Janet. "Please, I need to talk to Shea. I know everything." Pulling the crumpled letter from his pocket he gave it to her.

Janet read the document carefully before handing it back to him. "I told her to let you help her."

"Where is she now?"

"She said she was going to talk to you. My guess is she's up on the hill."

"Thank you." Billy kissed her cheek before running out again.

◆   ◆   ◆

Shea pulled her car up and parked back in the woods. She sneaked around the side of the house and was relieved to see Billy's truck not parked in the drive. She figured as much, he was probably out looking for her.

184

Letting herself in with her key, she worked quickly to gather the things that belonged to her and Ben. She went into Ben's room first and looked through the drawers, collecting the clothes that had made their way up to the lake. They spent most of their time there now, so there was a lot of stuff to gather. She picked up the picture sitting on the dresser. It was one of her favorites, of Ben and Billy fishing together. Maybe one day things would be all right and she and Billy could finally be together. She'd miss him desperately. She knew she'd never be able to love again, but she couldn't stay, not with a madman after her son. Ben was all she had, and now she realized all she'd ever have.

She let the picture drop to the bottom of the bag and continued emptying the drawers. She dashed the blinding tears away and went to Billy's room. She slowly folded up the shirts and shorts from the day before, adding them to the growing mound.

The sun shone through the window like it did every morning. It warmed the room so that Shea opened the window. Listening to the commotion going on in the barn for a few seconds, she realized it wasn't the normal noise, something was wrong. She took the rifle from the corner of the room and went out to investigate.

◆   ◆   ◆

Shea entered the barn carefully, holding the gun in front of her. The horse was rearing up on his hind legs, kicking the stall. She ducked down and made her way to the gate. Unlatching it, she stepped back, allowing the horse free passage out. She fell back on her rear as a snake slithered by. It startled her, but she was relieved to see that was all that had caused the disturbance. Getting back up Shea went over to calm the horse, who'd trotted to the other end of the barn.

"It's okay." She inched her way closer, holding out her hand. He walked slowly toward her until his nose nuzzled against her neck. "Poor Sugar. That snake gave you quite a scare, huh?"

The horse was still shivering, so she rubbed his neck and talked soothingly to him.

"Hi, Shea," came a voice from the second stall.

Shea jerked. "What are you doing here?"

"I should be asking you that." The man cocked his head to the side. "You weren't by any chance getting your things so you could run away, were you?"

She glared at him. "That's none of your business. Nothing I do is your business."

"Oh yes, my sweet, I think it is."

"You are the lowest son of a bitch... I'll see you dead first."

Now that... would be interesting." He leaned against the door. "If you killed me, you'd go to prison for sure. You don't want to do that. I've been there, I know." He moved closer.

Shea lifted the rifle and aimed it directly at his head. "I have enough reasons to blow your head off right here and now. Don't come any closer."

"Go ahead shoot me," he sneered. "If your brave enough."

Shea cocked the gun. He reached over while her attention was diverted and snatched it away. "You ought to be careful with this." He pointed it back at her.

She stood rigid, casting her eyes for an escape.

"These are dangerous...pow!" Laughing he stepped back, putting the gun down behind him.

As he moved to scare the horse away, Shea made a leap toward the gun. She slid across the barn floor, knocking the gun over. The man spun around and grabbed it before she could get a good grasp. With a scream, Shea scuttled back into the corner. He sneered in contempt, walking slowly toward her with calculating steps.

"Now ain't this something. You and me alone again." He kneeled in front of her, reaching out to touch her face.

Shea kicked him hard with all the strength she could muster, landing a foot deep in his groin. Letting out a yell, she made a run for it. From his prone position, he reached out and grabbed her by the ankle, sending her plummeting to the floor again. "You bitch! I'll teach you!" Sitting up, he got the rifle and held it out aiming it directly toward her head. "Get up!" he ordered, hitting her leg with the barrel. She pushed herself across the floor to the corner where he was indicating, looking up into his dark eyes. With a terrible calm she knew she was about to die. All she had worked for to

186

escape this man had been for nothing. How had her life come full circle?

Shea's worst fear had been realized. She was crouching in the corner of the barn, staring into the eyes of the one man she feared and hated more in all the world. Her head was spinning and her body throbbed from their struggle. As Kevin approached, Shea tensed, ready to defend herself to the death if necessary.

"Why won't you leave me alone?" she hissed. "Why can't you just stay the hell out of my life?"

"You have my son. That makes your life my business. You may as well get used to it, the courts are going to make you let me see him."

"I'll kill you first, you bastard!"

"I'd like to see that," he smiled coldly, "considering you're in no position to carry out your threat."

As he advanced on her, Shea huddled in the corner, looking up at him. With a terrible calm she knew Kevin was about to finish what he'd started all those years ago.

◆   ◆   ◆

Billy saw Kevin's truck at the end of the road and pressed the gas even harder. Sam was close on his tail and Billy called the police on his car phone. He knew Shea was in serious trouble. He only hoped he could get there in time. He wondered if she even knew how dangerous Kevin was. He drove fast, leaving a trail of dust so thick Sam could barely see the road.

Kevin couldn't hear the trucks pull up over Shea's screams. He was attempting to rip her shirt off, but she put up a strong fight. She kneed him in the groin, which only made him more furious. He threw her down, slapping her hard across the face. Grabbing a handful of her hair, he flinched as she reached up and dug her nails deep into the skin of his face. He yelled out and slapped her again. She fought with a frenzy, biting and kicking. Her struggling excited him further; doubling his efforts, he slammed her onto her back, tearing her shirt down the middle.

Shea kept up her defense. She would die before she would let him take her again. She continued screaming until his strong hand clamped around her neck. She gasped for air, choking on the rising dust. Kevin shoved her face into the floor with both hands tightly wrapped around her throat. Feeling herself losing consciousness, she fought with everything she had to stay alert. She kicked at him again, but her legs didn't have any strength left. So, this was it, she was going to die. Ben's sweet face swam before her eyes and she gave one last ditch effort to free herself. She was able to push him off her, but he was on her again instantly.

The barn door swung open and Billy burst inside. Kevin looked up in shock, frozen in place. With a gun pointed at Kevin's face, Billy walked over and ordered him to let Shea go. Kevin resisted, but Billy warned him again.

"Get off her slowly," he said, holding the barrel of the gun to his brother's face. "You make one wrong move, I'll blow you away right here."

It took everything in Billy not to kill him there and then. Kevin rolled off Shea slowly.

She tried to scramble to her feet, but stumbled. Billy saw her distress. Keeping the gun trained on Kevin, he moved to help Shea. He pulled her back next to him.

"Oh, Billy!" she cried, "he was going to do it again."

Sam came through the door and Billy handed him the gun. Sam held it while Billy checked Shea. He dusted the dirt off her and examined the deep cuts on her legs. Shea leaned against the stall, trying to catch her breath while Billy investigated the red finger marks developing around her neck.

Of a sudden he whirled and lunged at Kevin. Grabbing his half-brother's throat and squeezed as hard as he could. "You fuckin' bastard!"

Sam tried to stop him, but he was out of control. Shea screamed, hurting her throat. "Billy, it's not worth it." She staggered over to him. "Stop!" she cried, "you'll go to jail! He's not worth it, please." She got a hold of his arm and pulled him away as best she could. Billy backed off and watched Kevin trying to get up.

"You don't understand, Billy," moaned Kevin, trying to steady himself on his knees. "See, she wanted it...."

188

Billy slammed his left foot across Kevin's temple. "Shut up!" Kevin winced. "You're going away for a long time, big brother." The sound of police sirens rapidly approached.

"For what? Nothing happened," gasped Kevin, holding his hands over his head against another blow.

"Try rape, for starters."

"You can't prove that."

"I just did. There's a lot more, big brother. Embezzlement, fraud... should I keep going?" Shea looked at Billy in surprise. "See, Sam here has been working for me," he continued. "He's been watching you for some time, now. Seems you've been doing a lot of funny things with the family business."

Two policeman charged into the barn. Billy stepped back to let them pass. "He's right there, gentlemen."

The police officers yanked Kevin's hands behind him and cuffed them. They roughly led him out of the barn.

"You're a disgrace to the family name," spat Billy as he passed.

Kevin looked back at him spitefully. "I'm not through with this family, yet. I'll get everything that belongs to me."

"Get him out of here," ordered Billy. He shook Sam's hand and thanked him for the great job he had done nabbing Kevin. Then he helped Shea out of the barn.

Sugar had trotted out into the barnyard and stood, still shaking. When Shea told Billy what had happened to the horse he decided to leave her out to calm down.

They walked around the side of the barn in time to see Kevin being hoisted into a patrol car. Sam waved and beeped as he drove off after the police. Billy walked Shea over to her car and they got in. He hugged her close for several minutes. He thought about the night before and how scared he was he'd lost Shea again.

He kissed her hair. "I was so terrified last night, Shea."

"I almost ran away again," she murmured, laying her head on Billy's shoulder.

"I was so afraid I'd lost you again. Shea, I don't think I could ever take that again. I not only almost lost you, I almost lost Ben. You two are everything to me."

189

"I'm sorry, Billy. Janet told me I should trust you. I was just so scared, I didn't know what to do."

"It's okay, it's all over now." He held her to him.

"Let's go get Ben," suggested Shea, after a moment.

Billy smiled at her as they drove down the old, dusty road. Traveling to their place in life where they would be together.

ℰPILOGUE

Jake Kendall struggled on his cane, stopping once to catch his breath. It was difficult for him to walk, but nothing would keep him away from what he had to do today. He made his way down the dark, gray corridor to the visiting room. The guard opened the door for him and Jake staggered in, heading to the table where Kevin sat, smoking a cigarette.

He sat down in front of him and drew some papers out of his front pocket. Not saying a word, he laid them on the table, pushing them toward his son. Kevin avoided looking at his dad or the papers. He twirled his cigarette in the ashtray.

"What are those?" he demanded at last.

"Adoption papers," Jake answered in a monotone voice. "Shea and Billy are on their honeymoon and I want them signed before they get back."

"What do you need me to sign them for?"

"Security purposes," he countered. "I want to be absolutely sure you have no rights to that child at all."

"He's my son," spat Kevin.

Jake took out a pen and threw it across the table. Kevin ignored the gesture, taking another drag of his cigarette. "Bringing these here really proves I'm right. Why should I sign?"

"He's not your son and you'll have nothing to do with him! Do you hear me? I still can't believe you did such a vile thing to that girl. Just because you planted a seed doesn't make you a father. Billy's his dad."

"You don't give a damn about me, Dad. Why should I care what happens to them?"

"They are part of our family. All of them."

"Seems everyone is member of our family except me," sneered Kevin.

"I've given you every chance to come back to us." Jake's tone was rigid.

"You never cared about me, Dad. At eighteen you shoved me off to the army. You made them send me to Vietnam! You never gave a shit, ever since Mom died you've done what you could to get me out of your life."

"Oh, stop the self pity. I treated you no different than any one of my other children."

"You only have two children. Me and Brenda."

"Billy and Michael are just as much my children. You never could get over the fact I married again, that's what all of this is about. Now you sign these papers or I'll make sure you serve so much time in here you'll never get out. You're still in my will, son, but I can change that real fast. Now do the right thing for once in your life. Sign the adoption papers. Let that boy have a decent father." Jake pushed the papers directly under Kevin's nose. "Remember you're still in the will," he reminded him.

Kevin hesitantly picked up the pen and put his signature on the lines that were highlighted. Jake took the papers back and put them in his pocket. "I'll make sure you have the best representation, son."

He turned and stumbled out of the visiting room, passing Sarah on the way. She shot him a bewildered look, then passed. She sat down across from Kevin with a sorrowful look on her face.

"How are you, baby?" she asked, putting her hand on his.

"What are you doing here?" he asked in disgust.

"I came to see you. I'm worried about you." She pulled her hand away and sat back.

"How are you feeling?" asked Kevin.

"Oh great, the baby's fine."

"Sarah, you don't have to lie to me. Naomi told me you lost the baby. Look, it's for the best."

He looked into her tearful eyes, taking her hands in his. "Sarah, forget about me. I'm going to be in here a long time. Get on with your life. Find someone new who can give you what you need."

"I need *you*," she sobbed.

"Sarah, I can't give you anything from here. Please go." He got up. "I'm sorry," he said quietly. Turning, he signaled the guard to let him back into the cell area.

Devastated, Sara watched him walk away without a backward glance.

ABOUT THE AUTHOR

Alison White loves the creative process that brings her characters alive for everyone to enjoy. Her years as a resident of upstate New York helped her create a setting meant for romance and intrigue. In support of her true love, writing, she researches her stories and characters by traveling across the country and studying history of all kinds. In her spare time she likes to travel with her husband and play mom to her Golden Retriever and Persian Cat.